THE LAST MUSEUM

ff

BRION GYSIN

The Last Museum

faber and faber

LONDON · BOSTON

First published in 1986
by Faber and Faber Limited
3 Queen Square London WC1N 3AU

Photoset and printed in Great Britain by
Redwood Burn Limited, Trowbridge, Wiltshire
All rights reserved

British Library Cataloguing in Publication Data

Gysin, Brion
The last museum
I. Title
813'.54[F]   PS3557.Y8

ISBN 0-571-13938-8

For I have been a boy and a girl and a bush and a bird and a dumb sea fish . . .

Diogenes Laertius, VIII,77

CHAPTER ONE
GROUND FLOOR
WEEK ONE
ROOM 8

Rap! Rap! Rap!
Knock! Knock! Knock!

'Let me in, it's cold as the grave out here!' I can hear myself crying as I pound on the narrow street door of the old Beat Hotel on the Left Bank of Paris in the Latin Quarter. 'It's cold as the grave and I'm out here all alone in the dark. Lemme in! Lemme *yinnnnn!*'

'Gnyaaa!' yawns the door without budging an inch. 'Go 'way!'

'Who said that?'

'Me,' groans the door. 'An' you, who are *you*? Whazya name?'

'I don't have to give you my name,' I snap back. 'I own this rotten old flea-bitten French rooming-house. I bought it up lock, stock and bistro. Open up!'

'Whazya name?' grates the door again. 'Nobody gets in without he gives me his name, his real true secret name. Whaz yours?'

'Secret name? I wish I had one. I'm the richest little boy in the world and I don't like to give out my name. My name makes things cost double, at least.'

'It's gonna cost ya the world to pass through *my* portal, sonny boy. So, gimme ya name. Cough up.'

'Well, the newspapers call me Little PG or Young PG Six.'

'I don' give a shit what the newspapers call ya,' groans the door. 'What we want is your real true secret name. Everyone has one. If you don't know yours, that's just ... plain ... dumb.'

'Fuck you!' I yell, giving the door one swift kick.

'Ouch!' it yelps. 'Violence won't get you nowheres in a hurry.'

'I'm gonna have you torn off your rusty old hinges tomorrow!' I shout. 'I bought this historic monument, the old Beat Hotel, to have it moved out to my Museum of Museums in Malibu where I've collected all the other great historic monuments in the world. Scattered over the big part of southern California I own, I've got the Sphinx and the Pyramids, the Acropolis and Versailles and the Louvre and all that pinned down along the San Andreas Faultline. You know about the Faultline?'

'Sure,' squeals the door, 'everybody does. When the great earthquake come, as it must, the whole state of California is goin' to slide off under the Pacific Ocean.'

'Only half the state,' I insist. 'And not one day too soon!'

'Ya gotta be jokin'.'

'I am not. This renowned rat-trap, the old Beat Hotel, is going to be set down next to the Agora of Athens which I have made into the shopping mall of a small town in Apollo County, California called Palmdale, Palmdale-on-the-Bulge, the first to go.'

'You don't *mean* that,' moans the door.

'I do. My magical movers, a reputable Swiss firm called Interdean International Movers, can do anything I tell them to do. They brought over the Great Wall of China for me to set down along the line of the Los Angeles aqueduct, out across the Mojave Desert past the Diamond Mountains to Death Valley.'

'That figures,' admits the door rather churlishly, 'but your Interdead Irrational Movers can't move you in here to-night unless you come up with your name and not just your number, Little PG Six.'

'I'm exhausted,' I whine. 'What I need is a good hot bath.'

'Yeah,' sniffs the door, 'you sure do. Phew! You're ripe.'

'If you mean I smell bad . . .'

'You do. All dead people do but I like it. I'm kinky that way. 'S only normal.'

'I had an accident back there,' I admit, 'but I'm just as alive as you are and I'm not going to take any more of your shit!'

'Shut up and stop screaming, willya. Nex' thing we know ya'all be wakin' the dead an' scarin' the the naybors. So, can it! Lemme tellya, I'm freakin' out too, I'm that lonely. Let's put it this way: I wanna piece an' you wanna peace an' I wanna you only. Ya follow me?'

'No, I don't but it does sound familiar. What kind of proposition is this, anyway? I don't understand you.'

'I don' unnerstan' myself, sometimes. That make ya feel better?'

'Is that an Ancient Egyptian accent you're trying to put on?'

'Yeah,' chuckles the door, 'howja guess? I am the Door and the Posts of the Door of the Ancient Egyptian Book of the Dead.'

'Have you been drinking or smoking or shooting or sniffing something?'

'Juss takin' what comes along natural, like you, f'rinstance. 'Cept, how could I know that the richest l'il old boy in the world would come along tonight wantin' ta get inta me?'

'You're making a big thing of this. All I want is a quiet night's sleep before they take out the hotel. I don't like the turn this conversation seems to be taking, sexually. I can't follow you, don't want to.'

'I'm a soft touch. Whyncha touch me. Juss cuddle up. Y'all see I'm hot stuff. Out here all night all alone, I get kinda horny. In my day, I seen lotsa young boys, booful young boys like you, take out their cocks an' piss on me. Thass wha' I really like . . . Golden Showers. Whyncha try?'

'I haven't needed to take a piss since my accident.'

'Juss take it out anyway. Maybe that'll help ya remember ya name. You want this hotel for your Museum of Museums because of that bunch of Beatniks who lived here, doncha?'

'Yes.'

'Well, they all knowed their real names. Thass why their names are up there in the street on the wall above your head, inscribed in gold letters on marble paid for by the Ministère de la Culture and La Ville de Paris.'

I took a step back into the street to look up and, at that moment, the heavy iron shutter on the bistro began to roll up very slowly, like the iron fire curtain in a theatre before each performance.

What it revealed was a scene I knew from old photographs taken back in the twentieth century before I was born, at least this last time. Of course it looked strangely familiar but rather dreamlike. Through the steamy etched glass window and door, through the lace curtains and the spindly aspidistra plants, I could see the grubby little old bistro like the set for a faded French black and white movie made when my ancestor PG One was alive. The name *J. B. Rachou* was painted on the glass door in the calligraphic hand of an old-fashioned master sign painter. I recognized little blue-haired Madame Rachou, herself, inside there jumping up and down like a bellringer as she put her whole weight on the pulley which raised the heavy iron shutter in short jerks. She looked like some sort of toy on a spring, and for the first time since my accident I laughed heartily as I put my hand on the door to open it as soon as she had raised the shutter sufficiently.

On stepping inside, when I put my foot on the crazy-tiled floor, I felt a slight wave of vertigo, as if I might fall into the pattern. I felt not quite sure where the level of the floor was. This gave Madame Rachou time to skip behind her celebrated zinc-topped bar and jump on to an overturned wooden wine crate. It gave her the elevation she needed to dominate her whole domain, not only the three marble-topped tables with slim cast-iron legs but the whole hotel, all forty-nine rooms on the seven floors of it. She could do this with the aid of her Light Control Panel. Facing the bar, next to a door with a glass panel through which she could control the narrow hall and the door I had been talking to, was a panel of electric switches. Under each of these was a small enamel plaque with the number of the corresponding room. Above each of these was a tiny flashlight bulb which lit up as soon as the light was turned on in that room. Furthermore, she could look through the door into her dusty dining-room which had a window giving on to the stairs and see at least the legs of anyone coming in or out. Behind her zinc counter, her short arms crossed over her pale blue dustcoat with a round smocked collar such as French working-class people wore every day except Sunday through the last century, she looked like a proper little tyrant if a kindly one.

'*Bonsoir*,' she greeted me, 'we were expecting you.'

'I wasn't even expecting to be here, myself,' I mumbled sheepishly.

'I'm afraid you'll have to wait a while for your room. That young lady got here just ahead of you. You recognize her, of course, she was in the same accident with you. She was hitch-hiking.'

A gigantic American chick with a backpack and a bedroll and God knows what all else piled around her seemed to have materialized at one of the café tables. I knew I had seen her someplace before but I said, 'No, I don't think so.'

One of the bulbs on the Light Control Panel began to glow and burst into nova before it fused and went out.

'That will be Room Eight for you, Ma'mzelle. It is being vacated. You,' she went on, turning to me, 'you will have to go into Room One.'

'I didn't know I had to go into any room,' I objected. 'You know who I am, don't you?'

'Of course I do,' she snapped, somewhat vexed. 'You will have to go through all the rooms, one after the other, except for Rooms Two to Seven on this ground floor which have already been torn out by your rather over-zealous Swiss movers. Even Room One should not be available. They wanted to take it out too but they had trouble trying to get the plaster ceiling down in one piece.'

'Because of the painting of the nude woman,' I nodded. 'I know all about that. I gave orders for them to take great care about that painting. My curator of French painting considers it a masterpiece.'

'Masterpiece, hmph,' snorted Madame Rachou. 'I don't

think it's decent. An insult to womanhood. If I had known someone was painting that on my ceiling, I would have put them out of the hotel.'

'I've only seen photographs,' I admitted, 'but some of my curators did find her a bit pornographic. They dubbed her The Open-Gate Girl. By the way, that reminds me, I should call my museum to tell them I'm here. Do you mind if I use the phone a minute? You can put it on my account. I've got to get through to the Coast.'

'That line is for local calls only,' she said a bit sharply. 'They know you are here.'

'How could they? I didn't tell anybody I was coming over to check out the old Beat Hotel. I didn't know I was coming, myself.'

'This isn't the old Beat Hotel,' she said, looking at me severely over the top of her steel-rimmed spectacles. 'This is the Bardo, the Bardo Hotel. You will spend your first week here on the ground floor in Room One. Take the key off the hook on that board by the door and cross the corridor. You will find yourself facing the door to Room One.'

Little used as I am to taking orders from anyone, I found myself doing as I was told. The hall was dark and dirty. As I passed it, I gave the front door a swift kick in its backside.

'Smart ass!' it snarled, 'You'll never get out of here alive.'

A big bed with a dirty sheet draped over it filled up most of Room One. Another dirty sheet hung over the window which gave directly on to the street. Room One must have been a small shop at one time because one wall was lined with empty shelves. I threw myself on the bed and looked straight up at the famous Open-Gate Girl with her tits hanging down like ripe canteloupes and her thighs spread wide apart. Her exposed vulva glistened like seafood. I was horrified to see that my pants were open and I was getting an erection. I remembered what my guru back in California had always warned me, that in the Bardo one must avoid welcoming

14

wombs and the temptation into the first dreary rebirth that comes along.

I sprang out of bed to pull back the sheet over the window because I heard chanting out in the street and there was the whole band of the antique Beatniks with their heads shaven like Tibetan monks wearing next to nothing at all. They have nothing much on but the skimpy off-the-shoulder orange robes of Buddhist brethren and it is snowing. Their noses are blue with the cold, icicles dangling. Their bare heads are shaved blue and they are handling long ivory rosaries of skull-shaped prayer beads, long as skipping ropes. Ginsberg and Orlovski and even Giorno can just about get by in this drag but on Burroughs wearing his very American hat and glasses it looks simply embarrassing. Kerouac looks kinda cute and so do some of the anonymous acoylytes and hangers-on who are earnestly passing around a community copy of the Bardo Thodol, the Tibetan Book of the Dead, handwritten on dried banana leaves and, in the act of doing so, destroying it. This gives me great satisfaction. That's the way I like to see them go. There is the very last copy of the Bardo Thodol which I bought from the very last Dalai Lama for a huge sum of money and it is dissolving into dust between their greedy fingers. I am delighted. This is just what I hoped would happen to it. I fall back on the big bed with my cock still sticking straight up, pointing into the twat of the Open-Gate Girl.

'I'm Suzi,' she smiles as she settles herself down on my cock with a very feminine flurry. 'I'm Number One Girl at the Sphinx,' she gurgles as she works it into her. 'I take care of the Specials, like you, you dear old thing you!'

'The Spinx?' I murmur.

'Yes, the Sphinx. The Sphinx is the Number One House in the world, in the Universe! And I'm Top Girl in the Sphinx, after Madame, of course. I'm the most expensive whore in the world. Madame sent me. Sends me to you. I can do every-thing for everybody. Age sex creed colour etcetera mean noth-ing to me but more money and more love, of course. I love Love. And money is nice too. It's that simple. Love is lovely. I love everything and more than anything, I love monsters like you, you know. People with a little too little of this or that or none at all or simply much too much of some other little thing like two fully developed cocks hanging down between their legs, or a hunchback, or something.'

'Ouch!' I cry, horrified, 'get the hell offa me, willya. Ya breakin' my balls and I never even heard of a man with two cocks.'

'I take care of the curious, the crippled and the careworn,' she insists. 'One crack out of my wise whips can bring down a government, ruin a country, start wars, change maps, wipe out the entire population of a continent if I wanted to . . . but I don't. I want only one thing and you know what that one thing is, don't you? You do, you do! It's you you YOU!'

'And I want you to stop humping me! You're hurting me.'

'You silly old thing,' she coos in my ear, 'why don't you let yourself go, darling . . . hmmmm?'

'Because I'm already gone, I guess,' I manage to mutter.

'Oh, come on! You can be utterly frank with me. Tell me everything, every last little thing. All your plans hopes fears ambitions and secret desires. There's nothing I don't know about men, nothing I haven't already been through with them, time and again. I've had millions and millions of men crawling at my feet throughout all of history. There's nothing we haven't seen at the Sphinx. We've had flagellations and crucifixions going on day and night for years, forever. We deal in bondage servage slavery humiliation mortification suffering torture disfigurement detention retention, you name it! We've got sacred prostitutes, consecrated nuns dressed up to here in starch on the front but behind their bare asses are hanging out for you to pinch or to stroke kiss caress suck penetrate and paddle but not to whip because a good whipping can put a girl out of commission for days if you break the skin. The Syndicate won't stand for it. Madame has to be very strict. We all wear 6-inch high heels and a money belt, nothing else during working hours. You come in off the street along the entrance hall through three sets of swinging doors that buzz as you pass them and there is Madame to greet you from behind the Cash Desk with her curls piled high on her head like a heap of gold coins. You buy your plastic chips with the Sphinx stamped on them from her and they are good for girls girls girls! A Gurl makes her own price with a customer who pays her in the chips she turns in to Madame at the end of her shift and gets credit for them at the Syndicate Store. No cash changes hands but you can get anything you want in the Syndicate Store, anything in the whole wide world. That's how I was able to commission this image of me I live on in, the Open-Gate Gurl, direct from the artist who painted it without even knowing what he was doing, of course.'

'I guess that goes for most of them,' I manage to mumble from under her muff which she has thrust in my face like a hairy wet mop.

'Yep, that poor painter's dead. Got cancer of the rectum and committed suicide. Say, just give me your tongue a bit, willya!'

''S lucky for me I don't have to breathe any more but I won't give you head.'

'Wow! Wonderful! That's it, you've done it,' she cries, 'now you're talking. You're doin' swell, just keep that up.'

She is humping me like a sex-maddened sea cow I saw once as I sailed past on my yacht while she was jerking herself off on a buoy in the Catalina Channel. Over Suzi's shoulder I catch a glimpse of a whole gaggle of school kids, shading their eyes as they press their little wet noses against the plate-glass window which gives on to Shit-in-the-Bed Street.

'Hey, there's some kids out there watching us. Lemme outta here, willya!'

'I'm coming! I'm coming!' she cries.

'But those kids out there! They got nuns in hot pants out there behind them. And cops. And someone who looks like my mother! Oh, wow!'

'That's our public,' she pants. 'Oh, I'm so excited, darling. I'm so glad for you. This puts you back in the picture.'

'Just let me pull the curtain a sec.'

'No, no, no! They have every legal right to watch. It's good for minors to attend the whole show and see all the Special Sexhibits. It's Museum policy, approved by the state laws of California.'

'What do you know about Museum policy and what's this Paris scene got to do with California?'

'Stoopid! Don't you even know where you are now? You're in the Museum and you gotta be glad of it. Men and boys will line up from here to eternity just to be laying where you are right now, babe!'

'You mean that as a transitive or as an intransitive verb, doll?'

'I wooden know, I owny work here.'

'Say, the whole room seems to be vibrating. It feels like an earthquake. Can you hear that rumbling sound?'

'Don't you just love it! That's only silly old Vesuvius, dearie, grumbling away as usual because we're having such a good good time in here. Aren't we? Don't pay it no mind. Sometimes at this time of day there's a quick rain of fire but it's only a shower and it clears out the crowd, tourists and holidaymakers. What's nasty are pumice stones as big as your head. They're so light they don't hurt much but they do pile up in the street something awful like pumpkins. You and I don't hafta worry about those silly old poison gases, do we, since we got no more need of breathing, anyway. The worst that can happen to us is that we get buried in that fine volcanic dust that hardens like plaster of Paris and we get sealed up in here, like in Pompeii or Herculaneum where the Villa de Lerium was once supposed to have been, if you can believe the word of your ancestor the Founder's architects and advisers. You see how the image can rise again and come back around again for a retread, you follow me?'

'Yes, I do and only too well. It's the very thing I want to make a break with, forever. Enough is enough! Let's have no more retreads, no more images of images of images. It's all done with mirrors. We want the real thing now and nothing but.'

'If you're so smart then, what is it, the Real Thing, according to you?'

'Enlightenment. Let there be Light.'

'Lava, liquid lava burning bright, that's the one thing we really do have to worry about.'

'Hellfire?'

'And brimstone.'

'Wow!'

'Yep, that's the lot. Let's get going again, shall we?'

'I can't get it up because of all those people staring in here.'

'OK, honey, forget it, but let's split before the ceiling comes down. I've got my Rocket on the roof. We can go for a spin in the country.'

Her Rocket on the roof is an out-of-date model and I don't much like the looks of it but I have to admit Suzi does know how to drive it. As soon as she ignites it and throws in the gears, you know that this pile is really hers, the way she handles it. We are flying low over Normandy, apparently, barely skimming over farms and tiled rooftops. Cows and even cathedrals loom up alarmingly only to sweep away under our exhaust. According to her control panel, we are travelling at twice the speed of light. She has one hand and elbow on the steering and the other deep in my crotch where nothing is happening, naturally.

'Where are we going?'

'This is my afternoon off,' she says. 'I asked Madame if I could take you to meet an old pal of mine who is nine years old going on ninety. A real little Buddha. But, then, everyone is having little Buddhas these days, aren't they? I don't want to boast but my little Buddha is something special. You'll see. Like you, my son's an Old Soul, of course. My son! Oh I know you two'll make out, get it on together. It's a real break for an Old Soul to score for a beautiful young body, you dig.'

At that point she was looking deep into my shallow blue eyes and just missed the spire of what looked like Chartres Cathedral.

'Suzi!' I yelp, 'you better watch out or we'll have another accident.'

'Accident?' she screams into the wind of the world. 'I

never had an accident yet. You're the one had the accident, Buster.'

'Don't look at me like that. Look where we're going.'

'This old contraption of mine knows its own way out here, knows its own way to the FUNNY FARM. You see, I just leave it on automatic. This old soft machine of mine, we've been over this trail together so many times, I can't tell you. My own little Buddha has been up here with the Tibetans ever since he was going on four. What happened was, I had passed out at home once on some bad stuff somebody gave me and when I came to he was gone. Just like that. No note to mamma. No nothing. Just picked up his skateboard and sailed away by himself up the highway and I didn't see him again for nearly nine months. Time enough to have had another one, you'll say, but since I was working at the Sphinx night and day I had my Fallopian tubes pinched off. I was beside myself with worry, you can imagine, barely able to get through the night-shift on the old workbench. Madame was very kind. She put me into Room One where I take on the Specials like you, my dear. I was into Tantric Kundalini and Tai Chi and Rajneesh and all those sorta sexual disciplines, so I could take care of it. I really dig working in One. Instead of being out on the parlour floor with the rest of the girls, I can meditate between clients. It's got so's I can use my meditation in my business. A shift goes by like a song and I draw down more money. Men are so silly. Lots of French businessmen and even Cabinet ministers always want to play Cock-a-doodle-doo or, as they call it in French, Co-co-ri-co! Can you imagine, they wanna play Rooster! I have a rubber cork with red white and blue cock feathers stuck into it which I ram up their asses after tying their hands behind their backs so they can go flapping around with an erection while I play the broody hen. It's all so very French, isn't it?'

'Suzeee! watch out where you're going! You just ran over a whole flock of chickens.'

'That musta bin the farmyard of the old château, I guess, so we're gettin' there. The old château is at the end of this long avenue of trees. Don't mind that noise this contraption makes, we're not fallin' apart. That's just my air-brakes. Ooops! That almost did it.'

As we sweep down the avenue of bare trees, I shut my eyes against the glare of the low winter sun hanging like a big billion-watt bulb setting between the evenly spaced trunks. They were planted at exactly the right distance apart and we are travelling at exactly the right speed for them to produce flicker in the alpha band, at between eight and thirteen inter- ruptions of light per second. Well-remembered galaxies begin to spin through my interior space, flashing in all their unearthly colours. I am delighted, naturally. It means that my EEG has not flattened out yet and the old brain is still work- ing.

'Just wish you'd shut up a minute.'

She is babbling on about her business as women will, boast- ing that she is the only whore in the whole wide world who knows how to provoke ultimate orgasm in the male by some fancy figure of love only she knows how to perform properly, called Napoleon on the Ramparts. 'Here we are. We have arrived,' she says. 'So there! Aren't I clever!'

And here is Burroon, William Siegfried Burroon, as I have suddenly decided to call him. I know him instinctively because I would never have recognized him from his pictures in my archive or his old movies Uklut and I used to have at home. And here I am home again. Whatever just happened? And how? It is almost too much for me. William is standing out on the broad front steps of our old château in the rain. His silver-rimmed glasses are glinting out from beneath the huge hood of a woolly Moroccan jellaba beneath which his pale and impassive old junky face looks like two ivory profiles stuck together. I stand there stockstill for a long minute. I don't know what it is but something really radical is happening inside of me. As soon as he speaks, I know what it is:

'You're looking good, Ion,' he says, 'in the, uh, circum- stances.'

He mistakes me for his young friend Ion Sommerville.

Now I know all about Ion Sommerville. I've studied up on him and his short life so I want to check at once to see if I have by some goofy mistake in transfer become poor Ion. Sommerville crashed his car, killing himself on the way back from the country post-office where he had just received a copy of a scurrilous personal attack on him by an ex-friend in Amsterdam. This article has a graphic description of his penis, its shape and size, so I flip down the codpiece of my space suit to check on it. No doubt about it, the cock in there is my own. Any man would know his own penis anywhere, now wouldn't he? After all!

Buroon is welcoming me into the old château, making it sound like this is his place more than mine. I laugh, knowing these old tricks of his and turn back on the driveway to see what has happened to Suz'. And there she is doing prostrations, full Tibetan prostrations, flopping around in a big mud puddle in front of a small red-headed boy of about nine, in the orange-red robes of a Tibetan monk. He is not making the least move to help her up. He just stands there with an angelic smile on his shining face and he is standing in the foot of a rainbow. As she embraces his bare feet the rainbow seems to cleanse her too. She needs it.

'That's my little tulku,' Buroon purrs in my ear as he lays a wooden arm over my shoulder. 'I'm teaching him the basic tricks, like how to deal with women. You gotta terrorize women, thass all. That talkative mother of his is a perfect pest, a real pain in the ass. C'mon inside.'

'That's a truly beautiful little manchild,' I say. 'And, may I ask, just what else are you teaching him?'

'Actually, I'm supposed to be teaching him English but in fact he is teaching me how to spell. You know what a sloppy speller I am. The only trouble with his English is he speaks it with that excruciating singsong East Indian accent. Otherwise, he knows more English grammar than I do. Knows the difference between a transitive and an intransitive verb, for example. More'n I do. Say, you feeling tired? Wanna go lay down for a while?'

'What I said was: what *else* are you teaching him, William? I know *you*.'

'Tut tut, young man, let's have no more of that kind of talk. I'd like you to remember you're in a monastery.'

'A monastery? It looks just like the old homestead to me, the place my great-great-grandfather Longfinger brought back stone by numbered stone from Normandy and set up on our spread out in Montana.'

'Maybe it is. I dunno, me. Thought it was a movie set.'

'It always did look like a movie set.'

'Maya, Maya! Doesn't everything? All is illusion. Everything is illusion except the chow, eh? But the chow here is terrible. Either it's putrid wild boar for dinner with the evil old Comte de Vile who owns this dump or else it's rice rice rice with the lamas. What I wouldn't give for a good bowl of chilli at Horn & Hardharts! Or a T-bone steak even better!'

'This is my private study in here.'

'Room Twenty-three, eh?'

'No, not really. We don't have numbers here, normally. I just chalked up 23 on the door, meaning: 23 Skiddoo! You'll see, the lamas have signs up all over the place, like: *Lamas' Dining Room* . . . and, *Lamas' Library*. On the front stairs it says: *Lamas' Staircase*. I have to go up the back way.'

'What happens when you get up there?'

'It says: *Lamas' Bedrooms No Admittance at any Time under any Pretext*.'

'But you get admitted?'

'I know what they're doing in there. For a long time I hoped they were at least fucking each other in the ass, down on all fours in a ring on the rug. But now I know better. They're just sitting in the lotus position in front of the television like anybody else.'

'Why do they have all those signs up?'

'To keep out the sneaky old Comte de Vile who is supposed to be handing the place over to them lock stock and barrel. On the one hand he really wants to give it to them to save his soul

23

but on the other hand he just can't bring himself to sign the papers. The lamas got some kinda psychic headlock on him but he's still kicking. Time is on their side and they know it. The Comte thinks they're in deep meditation in there and maybe they are. Who knows what you're really doing when you sit watching television all day and night? You don't even know yourself half the time.'

'Do you watch television, William?'

'Oh, I slide in there sometimes to sit with the lamas but you can't smoke. His Holiness suffers from asthma and that's that.'

'But isn't that a bit odd for someone like him to be suffering from asthma? I always thought asthma was psychosomatic.'

'When you've breathed the rarefied atmosphere he has breathed, my boy, it may not be at all surprising that the smog down here below on this level gives him asthma. When you come from the high altitudes he has known, you can easily be short of breath down here.'

'Now that I come to think of it, I don't know what's happened to my own asthma. It's gone, just like that.'

'And so,' Buroon observes gravely, 'so has your breath.'

'Yes, but I seem to be getting on with my second wind for a while.'

'For a while.'

'Tell me, how did you end up here, Bill, you of all people? Have you become a Believer? Do you really and truly go along with this Tibetan trip? Tell me.'

'Well, no, I wouldn't say that, not entirely. But, as I always said, you do have to take a broad general view of things. You see, my books weren't selling all that well and I was sick and tired of that lecture tour circuit. Never getting any writing done. All the time hopping in and out of airplanes. One damned faculty tea after the other with the faculty wives. Ugh! I like staying in all those good hotels for a while but that soon wore off. The whole thing was a drag and for not all that much money once IRS got its teeth in it. They're still on my ass for back taxes. They won't let you catch up. How can you? The more money you make, the more bread they want from you. It's a losing game. And then came this call. When I realized the lamas had set up a Buddhist monastery in the Normandy château your great-grandfather Senator Longfinger had brought over to the States stone by stone from France before World War One, how could I refuse? It was an offer I could *not* refuse, you understand me?'

'Oh, only too well!' I titter. 'William, you really amaze me.'

'The lamas invited me here for a Retreat and I retreated, thass all. What more can I say? I get along fine here. I like the lamas and the lamas like me. What more can one ask for?'

'I'm glad you feel at home here.'

'Right away, I had a flash with His Holiness. We stay in touch whether I see him or not. We stay in a state of constant communication, night and day. I'm in clover.'

'In *my* clover,' I insisted.

'In *our* clover, old man. Take it easy. You'll like it here, during the stay you been booked for.'

'In what used to be my own house!'

'Nobody can hold on to his own house forever. Besides, you always used to say youda burnt this place down behind you if you coulda. Why didncha?'

'Oh, I expect I can still learn something from the old homestead, even at this late date . . . even in my age and at my condition, as Madame used to say. English prepositions gave her a lot of trouble but I don't suppose they worry you, do they?'

'Ion, my boy, you have to take a broad general . . .'

'That's enough out of you, Billyboy. It looks like you are giving your wholehearted approbation to this Tibetan trip, are you?'

'At some point in life, one can do worse then attach himself to something big rich powerful ancient holy *and* smart.'

'But that sounds like the Catholics!'

'They're not all that ancient and the Church of Rome ain't all that smart.'

'Despite what you've always pretended, you're for Control!'

'Can't you just see the Dalai Lama in the White House?'

'Don't be absurd, William. You're . . . you're irresponsible!'

'Why not? What've I got to lose? For the moment, I got it made. The lamas have a sensory deprivation tank in the wine-cellars in which I can immerse myself for as long as I like with my little Tulku. The two of us just sorta, ah, slop in and outta each other for hours. I mean psychically. And is it ever tasty! You really must score for a young body while you're here, Ion. It brings back the memories.'

'I'm not all that interested in any mouldy old memories.'

'Well, if you can say that and mean it, my boy, you've come a mighty long way, let me tell ya!'

'I don't want memories. I want the real thing.'

'Uh, I don't rightly know just how much more of that you can have.'

'Well, what *can* I have? What else does this old dump have to offer? Tell me.'

'Oh, the Comte de Vile has his own shooting gallery in the basement and one of the finest collections of handguns in the world to practise with.'

'I know all that. I first learned to fire my pistol on that range in the cellar when I was a kid of eleven. I'd just learned how to do it. Me and Luke my Indian lover just my own age used to lie flat on our backs on an old mattress and shoot our wads at the twat of Suzi the Open-Gate Girl on the ceiling. We used to keep score. Without touching yourself with your hands, you had to ejaculate with enough force to spatter her thighs. Only two points if you hit her knees or her tits. Three or four points depending how low you hit on her belly. Five points for wetting her pubic hair. Six full points for a bull's-eye anywhere around the clock. Player disqualified for touching his cock with his hands or blowing down over the flat of his belly.'

Buroon laughs, briefly. 'I thought you didn't want any old memories.'

'Do I get to see Luke again? How long can I stay?'

'Not for long, I'm afraid. But make yourself at, uh, home, of course. I gotta cut out for a minute to see what His Holiness can do for you about a new outfit.'

'I could do with some clothes.'

'It's not just threads you need, boy, it's a body. I'll have to ask around, find what's available.'

'Oh, just any old thing will do to time me . . . I mean, to tide me over.'

'That was a very revealing slip, young Ion. Rash statements like that have a way of coming true, only too often. What we want for you is something eminently suitable, something perhaps better than your last deal, if possible.'

'Last time around wasn't all that bad. I got a square deal, I guess . . . after a fashion. One thing I learned for sure on that trip is that *any* body at all is better than *no* body at all. That's why people are so scared of dying, isn't it?'

Buroon just stares back at me stonily, eyeglasses flashing warning signals. Well, as I know William, I have no clear idea just what these signals mean. The hood of Buroon's Moroccan jellaba drops back of itself. He is wearing a little skullcap from Marrakesh with Arab letters woven into it around a ring of green bicycles. His ears seem to be quivering. He lights up from inside like an electric hotplate getting ready to fuse.

'We are terribly sorry, Old Soul,' says a singsong voice out of Buroon's mouth speaking with a very marked Anglo-Indian chi-chi accent, 'but we seem to have nothing available for the moment in the way of suitable accommodation for you, owing to the, ah, reconstruction work which the Museum is doing in the Bardo. You have seen the state of Room One. Rooms Two Three Four Five Six and Seven on the ground floor have been dismantled and shipped to Palmdale in California. You can perhaps profit from this, ah, anomaly in our arrangements by taking instruction. Someone on the other side is ready to give it to you. Look into the mirror on the door of the wardrobe.'

Turning to the mirror, I drop my sheet to see how the old bod has come through post mortem. To my surprise, I am about nine years old and I have a hard-on. Buroon's little tulku is in there smiling as he offers me a saffron robe. I can see it is the orange dressing-gown I once got for Christmas and never much liked.

'Luke!' I cry, slipping into it. It is icy cold out there on the old sleeping porch and snow is drifting in under the blue and white striped canvas.

'Oh, PG,' the other little boy laughs, 'that's your mother's name for me. You remember my real true name, don't you: Uklut?'

'Yes, of course, that's your own real secret Indian name, isn't it? Since I've been away at boarding school I almost forgot.'

'Never mind. Shall we begin the instruction?'

'Oh, I'm tired of instruction. What kind of instruction you got?'

'You should remember. After all, you were the one who showed me. For that body you got there to last through the holidays, it must be anointed all over with sperm.'

'Not in my hair! I won't get my hair wet and, besides, neither one of us can come yet.'

Uklut laughs. 'Just you wait!'

Thus doth he attain into the Station of Intimate Friendship (Khullah), in that he is permeated with the love of his Beloved, mingled with his Blood and his Flesh, both within and without, whence the necessity of wetting through and through (Takhlīl) the hair.

Takhlīl, Takhul (intimate penetration) and Khalil (legitimate pal).

'You really do love that little Indian boy, don't you,' I can hear my mother saying as she pulls my bare arms and legs off the familiar naked brown body I wrap them around every night, 'but I really do think that you and Luke should be wearing pyjamas.'

'But you went right on doing it, didn't you? Doing everything.'

'Not Takhul, that came later. He was my Khalil, though, always.'

'So, what did you *do* at that age?' Suzi insists.

'We moved out on to the sleeping porch in winter, in summer we slept in his wigwam but there was always his family about. You know, Suzi, sometimes you sound like my mother.'

'That's what I mean. What were you *doing* together? Who started, ah, "doing things" or how did you call it?'

'We called it that, "Doing things". I started it. After all, I'd had my first sex, if you can call it that, when I was four.'

'When you were *four*? How *about* that! Who with?'

'With a British colonial colonel in Brighton. Someone I met through my mother.'

'In Brighton, England? And how did that happen? With a colonel! What were you doing there with a colonel?'

'Oh, that's all too complicated to go into, babe. Anyway, it doesn't count since it all happened before my mother had both of us circumcised.'

'Circumcised? Who, you and the colonel?'

'No, stoopid, me and Uklut. I had an accident in the woods that winter I was eight, no, nine. I stepped into a trap. Out in the winter woods with Uklut, we fell on a trapline laid by some stranger, some interloper on the Longfinger reserve. That's how I got this funny left foot, like Oedipus. Our family doctor did a good job on it or I wouldn't be able to walk. Uklut hurt his hands getting the trap off my foot and he had to be operated on, too, in our kitchen. Nearly lost his hands, both hands.'

'In the kitchen?'

'In our huge family kitchen as dark as a cave full of steam and hung all over with white sheets, I remember it well, at seven o'clock on that winter morning when the doctor could get there on a horse-drawn sled through the snow. I was OK, more or less, but not poor Uklut. The night before, my Daddy gave me his last shot of heroin, at least he said it was his last. There wasn't enough for Uklut. Buckets of sweat were pouring off him all night but he never cried. I did, a lot. When the doctor came, he gave us all shots.'

'Daddy included?'

'Mummy too. How did you guess? She's the one pulled the castration number on us.'

'Castration? You've got to be kidding.'

'Well, circumcision. She's the one told the doctor to circumcise us both under the anaesthetic while he was fixing the rest. When we woke up, we both thought she'd had it cut off. We both woke up screaming because we were stuck together with dried blood and my mother was there, pulling us apart, saying, "I thought I told Luke's mother not to put the two of you in the same bed any more after your operations!" Thanks a lot.'

'Wow!'

'She said she had us both operated on because we were touching ourselves.'

'And each other.'

'Ah, yes.'

'And were you?'

'Of course we were and why not? You should see Italian mothers encourage their kids to pull at their puds. Helps 'em grow up, a whole lot.'

'And your mother, you never forgave her?'

'I didn't say that.'

'What did you say, there under your breath?'

'Maybe I mumbled something about blaming the doctor because of the heroin but my father gave us both more after that.'

'Your father? What happened to him?'

'Oh, he OD'd eventually and, later, my mother ran off with the man who laid that trap.'

'Who was he?'

'Oh, a veteran of one of those wars where they all came back junkies. He had a pension and he holed up in our woods. He was crazy, crazy like a fox. When they found him, he told my mother he was Lady Chatterley's trapper and that got to her, I guess. He entrapped her. It didn't work out, even at that.'

'Yeah, I'm glad I'm a girl but any girl's life is a trap, you can believe me. Look at our own relationship, such as it is. It isn't working out either,' said Suzi.

'I'm sorry about that, babe, but the heroin leaves me a little bit lame in the third leg, sometimes.'

'Is that why you haven't made love to me properly? Why did you bring me back here to this room in this sordid hotel? Don't you know who I am? I'm Special Suzi, doesn't that mean anything to you or don't you like girls, at all?'

'Hi, Suzi. Excuse me, but I think I'm going to take another shot to fix that.'

'Junk is no good, baby. Why don't you stop!'

'Why don't you stop talkin', babe, while I cook me this shot.'

'Kick that habit, man!'

'I'm kickin' it, I'm kickin' it! Juss you watch. Hope this doesn't upset ya, all this blood. I think I got a good vein left in my foot if I can only find it. This left foot of mine sure looks like an old fibrous root, don't it? I understand Lord Byron would never let anyone see his club foot. He took opium. Helped him a lot.'

'It's not helping you.'

'No, but this is better than O. It's Horse. At least, I hope it is. I scored for it last night down in the toilet of the Select where I picked you up.'

'I hear there's been some funny stuff floating around the Select recently. Hope you didn't pick up on some of that. They're talking about hot-shots and such stuff. You better be careful.'

'It's too late to be careful. This stuff has been stamped on pretty heavy but it's good stuff.'

'Why did you bring me back here if you like that stuff better than me?'

'Open your legs, honey, open them wide. No, wider than that. You see, you look just like the Open-Gate Girl on my ceiling. Look up, look up! Yeah, go on looking up, baby, while I line up this shot.'

A flash went off in my head just as soon as I put that needle in my vein. When I open my eyes, here is the good Doctor B hovering over me. We are back in the big kitchen of our old Normandy château in Montana. It is hung with sheets and full of steam just like it was when I came to from my operation. Buroon looks like Lady Chatterley's husband's doctor, right after World War One in the early twenties. He is speaking to me very severely, like a movie star.

'Young man, you have been very lucky to come back here. You weren't supposed to do that with the very first body His Holiness rustled up for you. How many spare human frames you think we got? Nobody told you to go slithering back to Room One again with Suzi. Partly because of the trouble you brought on yourself by having those other rooms on the ground floor torn out and sent off to California, you'll find yourself back here in the old nursery. You can sleep on the sleeping porch if you want to but there's to be no climbing out on to the roof to kill bats with a coal shovel, like last time. You hear me?'

'Where's Uklut?'

'Uklut is busy doing something for me, for a change. You'll see him later. I suggest you go upstairs and lay down for a while. Get some rest. Time-travel takes it out of you. You know your way around the house. Don't go up the front stairs marked *Lamas Only*, that's for the monks. Take these back stairs through the kitchen. Pick yourself up a clean sheet on the way through. If His Holiness has anything to convey to you, I'll, uh, communicate with you. Take a Long Sleep. Pleasant dreams.'

When I sit up on the operating table, I am not at all surprised to find Madame Rachou in charge of the kitchen, directing a whole bevy of pretty young kitchen maids in starched caps and aprons. They are all tittering because I have an erection. I know who I am. I am Young Master, sole surviving scion of an ancient Norman race, and I treat servants like serfs. I jump up to stride through my feudal kitchen as naked as the day I was born, crying: 'Cock-a-doodle-doo and Co-co-ri-co!' Smiling sweetly, Madame Rachou holds out a nightshirt of the finest French linen embroidered with a count's coronet and the arms of the de Vile family. As she drops it over my head, I turn my bare buttocks to her with a saucy flip of my hips. All the serving maids laugh and clap their hands to their mouths politely. Under my nightshirt, I stick out my fist like I had the biggest hard cock in the world in there and I charge into their ranks like a rooster. They cackle and scatter screaming with laughter, smashing piles of dishes, upsetting pots and pans. Madame Rachou claps her hands and sounds off like the Mother Superior at the Sphinx: *'Mes filles!'* she cries, 'Girls girls girls!'

I nip up the back stairs, flashing the full moon of my bright young ass at them all.

In the old nursery at the top of the back stairs, my old toys lie around just as I left them but they are covered with dust. They are drowned in dust as if a volcano had buried them in its ashes. I get a lump in my throat and the tears really flow when I recognize Mr Barigoud, the elegant golliwog I got so long ago in Brighton. My mother bought him for me just before she left me in the care of my flighty young nanny in that residential hotel in this dim English seaside resort, a long time ago. She laid it on me that his name was Very Good and that was what I ought to be too. Curious counsel perhaps, seeing how black he was. His skin was black slipper satin and his hair was Persian lamb fur. I loved him at first sight, announcing his name was to be Mr Barigoud. He was the same size I was and much better dressed. He wore a black satin swallowtail coat over a red satin doublebreasted waistcoat with gold buttons and a pair of long black and white checked gingham pants, while I had to wear skintight skimpy shorts. He had shiny black shoe-button eyes and a smile a mile wide. When I undressed him, I found he had a penis the same size as mine at that age but his was only a twist of black silk with taffeta testicles.

Today he has aged so much I can hardly recognize him. He

is slumping there in my child's rocking chair, so covered with dust it has turned his hair grey. His shoe-button eyes have glazed over and his smile has faded away. His elegant swallowtail coat has gone and so have the gold buttons on his red satin waistcoat which has been torn back to reveal a horrible hole in his belly. Was he gored by a bull or operated upon by the doctor? A roll of white cottonwool guts is hanging out of his left side. Did he bleed to death? Someone has taken off his checked gingham pants and pulled down his briefs to play with his penis and circumcise him or has he been castrated? Oh!

In a flash, I know who has been 'interfering' with him: the colonel, of course!

The colonel was the first man to 'interfere' with me, so no wonder I remember him! Besides, I can never forget him because he cheated me out of my fortune, my penny. Every day, that colonel came by our rooming-house in Brighton like clockwork to ask if he could take me for a walk along the seafront. Without my young Irish nanny, he added. The colonel liked little boys a lot, a whole lot and he came on like an Old Family Friend to the ladies. All the ladies in our family hotel loved him because he told them tall tales about his forty years on the Persian Gulf in the Service. He always wore a fresh red carnation in the buttonhole of his lapel and he had a bright yellow smile of long false teeth he said were made for him out of ivory by a Chinese dentist in Kuwait. The ladies fell into a trance when he told them Arab men are always red-hot and ready, clean as a whistle because they are circumcised later in life than the Jews who do it to six-day-old infants. The Arabs wait until a little boy reaches the age of reason when he knows what it is all about, a rite of passage between the world of women and the world of real men, and that is what they become, all of them, men, real men. The ladies laughed.

At tea-time, he begs the ladies to have their little boys circumcised if they have not done so already. When it is done about six or even as early as four, it is tighter and better sex later. He reaches under the tablecloth to run his hot dry old hand up little boys' legs and under their tight little short pants to feel what they've got, to check on them. He speaks darkly to the ladies to warn them against an unfortunate condition known as phimosis. What is it? What is it? they gurgle. He tells them. They all laugh hysterically when he hisses, 'Blind Meat!' He proposes to undress my golliwog, black Mr Barigoud, to see if he is a Moslem. I scream bloody murder when he undoes the drawstring of Mr Barigoud's black and white checked gingham pants to pull down his bright red bikini briefs, but the ladies are all rocking with laughter around the dining-room table in the English seaside hotel where my mother has left me.

The colonel knows what he is doing. He is an Old Hand. He can get away with murder and has, many times. For forty years, he was a Secret Agent in all those hot dusty Arab countries along the Persian Gulf. There was no oil yet in those countries and only ill-defined sandy desert borders along which they waged tribal wars since forever. It was the colonel's job to keep things like that. Playing off one Arab sheikdom against another was a perilous game, more like snakes and ladders than chess, but he had one great advantage: he liked what the sheiks liked, hunting with falcons and very young boys. For him, a boy over the age of thirteen was already an old man. He was a real chicken hawk. So, knowing the risks he ran, the British Foreign Office had him issued with an ampoule of cyanide fitted into a hollow tooth. If the worst came to the worst, rather than let down the side, he was to take it out and crunch it like an after-dinner mint.

On retirement, he came Home to settle in Brighton where they, the little working-class 'chickens', run wild and nice little lads of good family can be plucked as they paddle about in the shallows at low tide with a pail and a prawn-catching net. The colonel netted a lot. The ladies went lavender in the face with laughter when the colonel pretended to make indecent advances to my own darling golliwog. I just hugged Mr Barigoud to me all the tighter and screamed. The colonel said that since I liked black men, he was going to take me out on

Brighton pier to see 'nigger minstrels' playing banjos. I scowled and I growled, 'I no wanny!' but I was intrigued and, after giving something to my nanny, he took me.

When we were halfway out along the pier, the colonel pointed out to me the 'nigger minstrels' who were strumming banjos and singing to English people in deck chairs on the stony beach below, and I screamed. I yelled and I screamed with rage as I jumped up and down on the boardwalk, hugging Mr Barigoud closer to me and sobbing. I hated those ugly white men in striped suits and straw hats who had blackened their faces with shoe polish right up their piggy-red eyes and down to their turkey-red necks. I was flying wild into hysterics but the colonel shot me down in mid-air when he swooped to snap his bright yellow teeth at Barigoud, taking a bite at his silky snub nose. I was horrified. That shut me up. He gave me a big black Queen Victoria British penny for shutting up and then a second penny to have my fortune told later, he said. Holding me firmly by one wrist, he dragged me on out to the end of the pier where he steered me into a bathing cabin and shut the door behind us. It was dark in there. Nothing abnormal about that, the colonel snarled, he knew all about little boys in the dark, he said. He knew them like the inside of his pocket. He tried to push one of my little paws in there to prove it while he pulled down my pants. I said I had no need to go to the toilet. Never mind that, he said, as he pulled what looked to me like a gopher out of his pants and tried to make me put my hand on it. It was purple and hairy and it jumped. So did I. He grabbed me by the back of the neck to try and make me kiss it with my little wet rosebud mouth.

I let out one ear-splitting squeal and the gopher dropped dead, shrunk up. In my struggle, my first penny for shutting up dropped through the floorboards down into the sea below and was lost. The colonel was furious. He grabbed Mr Barigoud and shook him until the fortune penny dropped out of his red satin waistcoat pocket into which I had put it, and the colonel pocketed it even before he buttoned up. While I was still screaming, he opened the door and pushed me out on to the deck of the pier where the upper half of a fortune-telling gypsy lady sat in a glass box. When you put a penny in her slot, her eyes began rolling around in her head under her turban, jingling her gold earrings as she raised a palsied wax hand with a pen in it and began to write a jerky script on a card in front of her. When she had finished, the card fell into a slot and slid out in front of you. The colonel grabbed it and began reading it aloud because I did not read very well since I was only four. The card read: *You will be happy all your long life, with lots and lots of children but no wife.*

I began to crow with joy at this good fortune but the colonel screamed louder than I could, saying, 'This is not YOUR fortune. This is MY fortune. You lost your fortune penny between the floorboards, so shut up. You just shut up. I'm taking you home, now, you hear me? Shut up!'

I couldn't wait to get home. Since it was my shutting-up penny that had fallen into the sea, I could not wait to tell my nanny who told my mummy all about it when she got back. When the colonel heard from my mummy, he fished out his hollow tooth and unscrewed it. Screwing up his courage, he popped his capsule of cyanide into his mouth and crunched it like an after-dinner mint. But that was not, as he had been led to expect, the end of that. He fell back into his bed writhing in agony and he went right on writhing and moaning all night until he passed out. In the morning, his charwoman let herself in with her key to find him on the floor, wallowing in a pool of black and bright yellow bile laced with blood. He was blue in the face with a mouthful of bloody feathers from having eaten his pillow after biting through the veins of his wrist. The char waddled out to call the Pakistani doctor down the street. The Pakistani doctor came and sniffed at the colonel, recognizing the smell of cyanide at once. When the colonel came to, the doctor began asking questions like: Where did you get the cyanide? Have you ever been or are you still a member of the British Secret Service? Are you connected with the British Foreign Office or any other?

The colonel managed to keep a stiff upper lip. He had eaten

away his whole under-lip during his night of agony. 'Don't know what you're talking about,' he managed to mumble, 'never heard of any such thing in my life.' The Pakistani doctor took care of him but when he got better he discovered that he had not really recovered, not quite. He could no longer achieve orgasm, let alone get it up. For him, life without sex wasn't worth living. When he got well enough, he popped up to London to see a chap he knew in the Foreign Office from the old days to complain that his capsule had not worked and he wanted another. Deuced bad luck, old chap, terribly sorry and all that, but FO ground rules lay down that cyanide capsules can be issued only to active agents in the field. Can't possibly imagine why yours didn't work. Jolly bad luck and all that but you know the rules of the game. Better luck next time, or perhaps I ought not to say that. Just carry on as best you can. After all, there are other things in life besides sex, old man. Take a cold tub every morning. Jog along the seafront since you're lucky enough to live in Brighton. Damned if I could afford it on *my* pension. Seabathing in winter might help you a lot.

Back in Brighton, the Pakistani doctor plays hard to get. Can't give you any more cyanide. Contrary to medical ethics, you know. I'd have to sign for it. Dangerous for me, expensive for you. How much would it cost? Quite a lot. How much? More than you can afford, no matter how rich you are, colonel. No, tell me! Tell *me*, colonel, how much have you got? You say you have no heirs, so why not give me the lot? To hand over all he owned to the Pakistani doctor almost killed the colonel. Very unfortunately for him, even the second capsule did not. My nanny told me all this. I never heard any more about him. I was much too busy learning to read and to write.

'Poor Mr Barigoud, poor dear old Mr Barigoud,' I murmur as I dust off my black brother tenderly, setting him straight on my childhood rocking chair in my old nursery. With the long middle finger of my right hand, I poke the cotton batting back into the hole in his black satin belly, pulling his faded red satin double-breasted waistcoat over it, tight. In doing so, I feel something hard in one of the pockets. What I fish out are two tiny glass capsules. Are they capsules of cyanide? I look at them in amazement. How could that have happened? My mind does a double back flip. I look around wildly, my eye falls on the old gypsy fortune-telling wax lady in her dusty glass case. Jumping up, I run over to her to slip an old blackened British penny into her slot. I hear a whirring sound, as if she were stripping her gears, and I'm afraid she isn't going to work but her hand starts to tremble, her earrings to jingle and her black eyes roll around knowingly in her head. I can see, now, that her so-called 'writing' is a fake. She deals out a store of pre-written cards which someone else wrote for her. Her dead hand holding the pen never touches its inkless point to paper. Her 'writing' is a joke, sometimes a bad joke. The card that drops out into my hand reads:

Barigoud did it. Barigoud is the guilty one. Barigoud must die. Barigoud . . .

I can't read the rest. The card drops from my fingers. I grab my old golliwog and shake him until the dust flies out of his Persian lamb hair, turning it black and glossy again. As the dust flies, his black shoe-button eyes take on their old shine again. His famous smile a mile wide flashes back. But I am not about to be won over as easy as all that. I am mad, insane, crazy, wild. I believe he did it. Because I have it in writing, I have to believe in his guilt. I don't care if it doesn't make any sense: I have it in black and white in front of my eyes. It must be the truth because it is written here where I am reading. Not just his black truth and my white truth but naked Truth herself is here, in calligraphic black on white. I would like to see it in print, too, because maybe I could make out the rest of the words, but just these are enough to inflame me against him. Barigoud must die, they say. I have to believe them. Print. They're in print!

Did he fall or was he thrown over? Did he fall from favour or was he thrown over for somebody else? Or how *did* it happen? Leaning over my narrow slippery terrace as far as I dare, I see him still falling falling falling to die broken down on the red rocks of Death Valley above whose clouds I had my Interdead Movers set the castle of the Old Man of the Mountain, Alamout. Nobody else saw him fall, but the State troopers discovered his broken body. Until then, nobody knew I had a black lover since childhood. I used to take Barry with me in my helicopter for long weekends up in Alamout. We smoked up clouds of hashish from Iran and often hallucinated. We lay around in a trance, or we played games like Russian Roulette or William Tell, or we played head games even more dangerous than that. Barry was deep into magic and we had seances. For eyeball to eyeball confrontations on the subject of Control, we called up the OM and PG One, my ancestor the Museum Founder. Old PG was a piker. I have been called a Sorcerer's Apprentice but the truth is, I know a lot more than he ever did. Hassan-i-Sabbah is something else.

According to legend, the Old Man of the Mountain, Hassan-i-Sabbah the Master of the Assassins, had his boys so well under control that he had only to lift a finger and point it at one of them without a word for that one to leap to his eternal reward down on the red rocks thousands of feet below. Ambassadors from great powers and intrepid lady journalists who were already mountain-sick and suffering from vertigo, were immensely impressed by this parlour trick of his as they grovelled with fear and clung to the crumbling edges of his narrow slippery clifftop terrace, shitting themselves in their pants. He needed to do it only once, of course. It's been re-broadcast ever since. Apart from this one demonstration of his control, he kept the media out of his castle. I was not so lucky. The death of Barry Good broke the barrier. The gutter press got on to the story that we were playing Hassan-i-Sabbah and all I had to do was to lift a finger for him to leap to his death.

The media massacred me when they made it a love story. There was only one way out. Somebody somewhere wrote, quote unquote: 'There is but one truly serious philosophical problem and that is suicide.' I don't know about that but there was only one way out. I ran out on to the sleeping porch where a seal-sleek head of shiny black hair was lying on the pillow.

'Uklut! Uklut!' I cried, 'I've got them! Two capsules of cyanide to crunch like after-dinner mints!'

When I come around again, here is Buroon again, hovering over me. He looked more than ever like a nineteenth-century country doctor at the deathbed. 'Ion, Ion!' he keeps calling me. I know very well I am *not* Ion Sommerville.

'I am not, I am not,' I go on repeating under my breath. 'I am not.'

'There,' he says, 'that's just it, exactly. Your first week here has run out and that makes a couple more young male bodies you've gone through in the short time you've been out here with us in the old château. Whatever are we going to do with you? What next?'

'Yeah,' I manage to murmur, 'what next?'

'I'm afraid you're not going to like it but the fact is His Holiness has no more boy bodies to hand. I'm terribly sorry, but I'm afraid you'll have to double up with Iona.'

'I'm a week here?' I mumble. 'I'm weak.'

'Yes, you should have spent the first seven days in the Bardo, but since, thanks to you, young man, all the rooms on the ground floor have been torn out and sent off to California with the exception of Room One, His Holiness has been kind enough to allow you to stay on out here until the time comes when you must move on upstairs one flight to Room Eight. The time has now come. You'll find Room Eight at the head of the stairs to your left. Since your own museum people rather maliciously reserved it for you in advance, you'll find it already very fully occupied by a female entity called Fiona.'

'Her name was Iona a minute ago.'

'Iona, Fiona, what does it matter? You museum people meant to give her your job.'

'My job? I don't have a job! My life has been my job.'

'That's just it. That's why you'll have to share the space with her.'

'How big is this space, is there room there for both of us?'

'Of course not. You'll have to get into Fiona.'

'And become a real girl?'

'Well, I don't know about that. You'll have to see. Room Eight has an iron-barred window on the staircase. She'll be in there, expecting you. If things don't work out . . . and I don't say they will because there's no real reason why they should . . . don't blame me, my dear. Blame yourself.'

CHAPTER TWO
FLOOR TWO
WEEK TWO
ROOMS 8 to 14

Naturally, I recognized PG Six as soon as I saw him down-stairs in the bistro of this dreadful so-called hotel. I always wanted to come to Paris but little did I think I would end up in a dump like this. Or Little PG Six, either, for that matter. Oddly enough, he did not seem to recognize me but that was just like him. Not only are we distantly related, connections by marriage on my mother's side, but I was a deputy assistant cu-rator in the GG and GR section of his gargantuan Museum of Museums, the Glory that was Greece and the Grandeur that was Rome Department, as he called it. The Museum, the MOM, actually sent me on a field trip to Delos from where I brought back the classical Apollo which he thought looked so much like him that he had his hair done that way, the poor fool. He never much liked me, pretended I did not even exist. My mother always said the whole family was like that.

He was a born-again Beatnik, like his father PG Five and his grandfather PG Four. His enthusiasm for the archaic Beatniks is what got us both into this fix. In committee, I voted against his plan to cart this rotten old Beat Hotel to Palmdale and set it down by the Agora of Athens which comes under the GG and GR. When the head of the department suggested I take my sabbatical a year early I knew what to think, so I decided to hitch-hike through Europe alone with my rucksack and my bedroll on my back. My big mistake was dropping by the Beat Hotel to see how the work was going. Back in California, my guru must die laughing. She warned me this was a trap and she is always right.

Madame Rachou told me this was the girls' floor. The front hall and the circular staircase with open pit Turkish toilets in

43

the wall between landings were bad enough but I knew I was trapped as soon as I pushed my way into Room Eight. With my very first step, I plunged my left foot into a battered tin pail of some nasty liquid that splashed up my thigh to my crotch. I have not been able to get this old pail off my foot the whole week. Room Eight is a narrow cell with one iron-barred window on to the staircase up which drifts the smell of those terrible French toilets. When I gotta go, I go clumping down with my pail on my foot. It is really a wonder that nobody seems to hear me. Now, all the girls on this floor are after me because I simply cannot make out how French toilets work. Trouble is, there's no toilet. It is nothing more than a hole in the floor above which is suspended a cast-iron cistern full of water with a dangling chain. You pull on the chain and Niagara Falls falls on you before you can jump out of the way as it goes roaring on down the stairs.

What I do is, I creep out when nobody is around very early in the morning and I leave my calling card on the stairs where it will get swept away when somebody else reaches in, pulls on the chain and the Niagara comes rushing out. By then, I am safely back in Room Eight, peering out between my bars. None of them seems to see me. It is strange, but this has often happened in my life and it goes on, apparently, here in the Bardo. There are some mighty strange Old Gurls on this floor.

'*Shiiiiit!*' shrieked one of them they all call the duchess, as she skidded down the stairs, right under my nose, '*Sheeeeey-iT!*' And then she added in a very American accent, 'Excuse my French. I meant to say, "*Merde*".'

She was my first victim and then came her room-mate, a Chinese lady army general, it seems. Then, an over-married American lady whose girl Friday is a Hungarian countess of ill repute, said to be a vampire. What next? The others followed suit until, at long last, I solved my own toilet problem. It was mainly the problem of the light switch, how to get in there and close the door behind me and switch on the light. What a miracle! Let there be Light and there was. The secret is simple. There is *no light switch*. How very Zen! How very French! They

44

do it this way to save 2 cents a day on the light bill. What you do is step boldly inside in the dark. When you shut the door behind you, you fumble around on the back of the door for a butterfly bolt. When you turn it, that shoots the bolt into a hole in the door-jamb where it makes contact with 220 volts AC and you better be careful. 220 volts AC can kill you if your hands are wet. No matter, that turns on a feeble 15-watt bulb. When you have done your business, you will find some torn scraps of a newspaper on a sharp nail in the wall. So, do not – REPEAT, do NOT – pull the chain overhead until you have stepped out on to the stairs.

The first time I managed this, it was along about midnight and I stepped out of the can to find myself pinned to the wall by the concentrated beams of several police flash-lights trained on my quivery body by all the Old Gurls on my floor. I was blinded, terror-stricken, scared shitless, if I do say so myself. I recalled being cornered one night in the Greek Gardens on the outskirts of Palmdale in California by a squad of nightriding Dykes on Bykes. And here it was going to happen all over again. Oh, no! I tried to shrink back into the bogs to pull the chain which would cause the waterfall to fall on the 220 volts AC and electrocute me before I was swept back down the stairs to oblivion.

The spotlights began dancing all over me in rhythm and all the Old Gurls broke into their anthem:

VEE VEE VEE!
YOU 'N' ME
WE'RE THE GURLS
UV VICTORY!
YEH YEH YEH!

Suddenly the hall lights went on and they all broke into cheers: 'Welcome, welcome out of the closet, the watercloset and the closet of Room Eight! Welcome, welcome, it's never too late.' And there they all were: the duchess and the Chinese general from Room Twelve at the head of the stairs. The door

45

to their room behind them was open and it was sparkling with candlelight inside like a great reception room in a French château. The Transylvanian countess and the American lady from Forest Hills were drinking out of a bottle of Jack Daniels they raised in a toast. Madame Rachou was a dream in blue, blue dress and blue hair. The Moroccan lady was wearing a glittering gold caftan down to the ground and there was another strange couple I had seen someplace before in a photograph perhaps. Of course, it was Gertrudnalice dressed in a very well tailored sackcloth and ashes over hip-high rubber boots. I was thrilled. They came down and carried me up. It took all of them together to get me off the ground.

This reception took my mind off the last thing I had seen in the toilet when I turned on the light. It was some graffiti on the wall right opposite me when I squatted down. It said:

DEMUESTRE SU CULTURA! DEMONSTRATE YOUR TOILET CULTURE YOU NAMELESS ASSHOLE!

signed: William S. Burroughs, Paris 1960

Madame Rachou was murmuring introductions in French: 'Madame la duchesse de la Farce . . .'

'Just call me Freddy. You're an American, my dear. Where are you from in the States? I'm from Massachusetts myself. Born Frederica Forshew of Pride's Crossing, Mass.' She has a very busy whisky voice and a silky black moustache.

'Frederica Floorshow,' sneers Elaine, adjusting her flaming red wig.

The wiry little American duchess has to be restrained by her oriental buddy, the imposing inscrutable Chinese general in full dress uniform with decorations. Then, in a flash, Whang has changed back into battle dress with an armful of service stripes, while Freddy is wearing a very butch pair of white satin coveralls with YSL embroidered on the breast pocket in gold. Very poor taste.

Madame Rachou goes on in English: 'And this is Colonel . . . no, excuse me . . . General Whang.'

46

The general clicks her heels and salutes.

'Whang and I have stuck together through thick and thin,' roars Freddy, 'ever since the Boxer Rebellion. My father, Fortescue Foreshew, was our Minister Plenipotentiary to the Forbidden City, Fortescue Foreshew.'

'Forescrew Floorshow,' mutters the lady in red, still trying to get her wig straight on her head.

'*Elaaaaaine!*' growls her bosom buddy in her velvety thick Transylvanian accent but trying to sound 100 per cent USA: 'Can it! Can it, for the love of Mike!'

'Who's this Mike?' Elaine growls back. 'You been cheating on me with some new mother called Mike? Where you meet up with this Mike, eh? Lemme at her!'

'That woman is dead drunk and beneath contempt,' snaps the duchess. 'People from Texas who . . .'

'Now, you juss watch out what you say about people from Texas.'

'Shut up, Elaine! You're not from Texas, you're from Forest Hills.'

'Like the Florsheims, the shoe people. What's so wrong about that? They never changed their name to Foreshew. I know they didn't. I maybe grew up there but I did marry a millionaire from Texas . . . a couple of 'em as a mattra fack.'

Madame Rachou sails on, smoothly introducing an obvious bundle of trouble, a veiled lady with eyes as black and slippery as watermelon pips: 'This is our little Lalla Shereefa from Morocco.'

'Lalla means Princess and Shereefa means I'm a saint, a hereditary saint since the Prophet. You can kiss my hand if you like.' She holds up her pudgy little blue-tattooed paw as high as she can for me to bend over and kiss it. When I can't get myself down to it, she insists, 'Go ahead, kiss it. It won't cost you nothing. It's my lucky hand. Good for you.'

'And this is Ms Elaine Waterbree from Texas. She knows many of the trustees of the Museum including Madame de Lemon.'

'Oh, I know *her* all right! I was disinvited to one of her

47

fancy dinner parties once. While I was still dressing, her social secretary phoned to say I was disinvited. I went anyway. My dear departeds weren't really rich enough or I'd be a trustee right now. Or I would have been. This is my buddy from Outer Transylvania where she used to be called Countess Bathory.'

'Not *the* Countess Bathory,' breaks in the duchess, 'not Countess Erzavetta Bathory? We all thought you were dead ages ago.'

'Well,' Poochie grates between her teeth, 'and how about you?'

'With a stake through your heart,' Freddy insists, 'buried under a crossroads.'

Poochie grins, baring the longest canines since Dracula from whom she is said to be descended according to Freddy who knows all about the European aristocracy from away back, how her family were all vampires because their ancestors were fierce nomads from off the Russian steppe who drank blood from a vein in their horses' necks while they galloped nonstop into Vienna. It made my American blood run cold but her room-mate defended her: 'Poochie was liberated from her own castle by American troops and exonerated by a War Criminals' court in Heidelberg after she married Staff Sergeant Pikestaff. I won't hear a word said against her and I won't have any of you girls calling her Poochie, either. That's my own private name for her.'

'Isn't she jealous,' simpers Poochie as she turns her wolfish grin on me. She has a certain charm, I must admit.

'These ladies,' sighs Shereefa, 'they fight fight fight! Always fight.'

'Oh, that's not *all* we do,' Poochie insinuates, leering at me in a very overt manner, smacking her lips. 'I work in a blood-bank.'

Madame Rachou brings us back to our senses. 'Girls girls girls!' she cries. 'You all know, don't you, what we are here for?'

'Yes No What?' they all cry together. Gertrudnalice was the

one strong single voice saying, 'Yes, yes, of course.' The rest of us were saying, 'No' and 'What?'

'We are here to go.'

'To go where?'

'To California.'

'I've just come.'

'You're not supposed to do that. Relax. Freddy says, relax.'

'Why California?'

'When?'

'We have just six hours left,' she says, 'and they may be very short hours indeed. Things have piled up here in the Bardo, thanks to the Museum. You may not have any more than an hour apiece to take Fiona through the remaining six rooms on this floor.'

'I take it these are orders from higher up,' observed Freddy.

'Exactly. Men are coming at midnight to dismantle these rooms for shipment to California.'

'Men? Who said Men? We won't let them! We'll fight them off, tooth and nail!'

'California? Thazz nodzo bad. I wooden mine California. Howz about you, Poochie? Juss lay onna beach or get inna movies, why not?'

The phone starts ringing downstairs in Madame Rachou's bistro and she runs down to answer it. It was her turn, I guess. She skids in my business. That's what my Mom used to call it. Every day three times a day she'd say to me: Fiona, have you done your Monkey Business? I was daydreaming of Mick and the Monkey Shiners when Madame Rachou came back to say there had been a complete change of plan to avoid the Interdeadinternational Movers who were already on their way. We were to pull up stakes immediately and move off in formation to Antonia's.

'Antonia Longfinger's house down the street?' queried Freddy. 'You must be joking! You don't mean it. How on earth or off it are we going to get there? I thought none of us could pass back through the mortal portal again.'

'Nor can we,' Madame Rachou agreed, 'but I'll show you a

way through a trapdoor in the floor of the bistro. Beneath it is the hydraulic lift for getting tuns of wine up from the cellar. A floor or two further down and we come to our little underground river, La Chie, which will take us down to the landing under Antonia's house on the river. There is to be a big party for her return from Japan.'

'How divine! How simply divine. Life was a party and here death is going to be a party too! I've always heard about Antonia's under-go-round little river. How she used to run on about it! Said she was going to write a book about it. I didn't realize she still gave parties.'

'It's a party for her book and at the same time to celebrate her hundredth birthday. All the Gurls have been summoned throughout history.'

'We must take her a present. What can you possibly give somebody who already has absolutely everything? Something fragile, a friend once suggested.'

'Fiona,' suggested Gertrudnalice as one woman, one voice.

'Fiona's not as fragile as all that but maybe. Anyhow, I'm simply dying to see Antonia again.'

'You not dying, duchess, you dead. Ha ha ha!'

'Don't be spiteful, Lalla Shereefa, so are you. By the way, how did you . . . ah . . . get here, yourself?'

'Too big party in palace. *Bang bang bang!* Everybody dead. Not all all but too many! Too many! My cousin the King, he OK. *Hamdullah!* Thanks God!'

'What a coincidence! General Whang here and I were at His Moroccan Majesty's birthday party in the Bahia palace in Marrakesh but I don't remember seeing *you* there. So many of our best friends were killed. An unforgettable party.'

'Yes, too many peoples. All dead. Where you go? Down by swimming pool?'

'Yes, where the diplomats were, by that big buffet with delicious Moroccan food. Pigeon pie, mm mm! Whang and I dove into the pool to escape the bullets. The water was red with blood.'

'Mmmmm!' grinned Countess Bathory, 'tasty, it was tasty!'

'Ooooh, I not go down there! Too many mens. Better up-stairs with girls.'

'But I understand that even up there in the harem . . .'

'Yes, one beeeg bomb! Taka lotsa nice girl. Too bad.'

'Was Antonia at the party?'

'Of course not. Antonia was in Japan taking care of her . . .'

'I've always wanted to meet this Antonia Longfinger. You know who she is, don't you Poochie? No? Well, neither do I but I hear she's about as glamorous as they come. You know who Antonia *is*, doncha? No? Well, neither do I, so there.'

'Oh, Antonia really *is* glamorous. She *truly* is: TRULY!'

'You *know* her, yourself?'

'Not all that personally but I've heard so very much about her that I feel I do. And I've heard but pull-lenty! She's richer than any of those people in Texas, reeeely! She's am-MAZ-ingly rich, she is reeeely!'

'Is she a Trustee of the Museum? That's what *I* wanna know.'

'But of course! Naturally!'

'You know what she IS, don't you?'

'Whaddya mean? *Sessshally*?'

'She's a nun.'

'A *NUN*? No! You gotta be jokin': don't take me for dumber than I am . . . not a *nun*!'

'Yes, a Nipponese nun and she has her own monastery in Japan.'

'You mean a nunnery, don't you? A convent?'

'No, I mean a monastery for girls. Antonia is the Mother Superior, the Abbess, and she recruits hundreds of them. All she can handle. And as I understand it, she can handle a whole lot. It's run more like a barracks. The nuns are armed. Antonia drills them for hours every day, I am told.'

'Say, thass groovy! I like Tiddlywinks. Less all go by Antonia's right away.'

'Girls girls girls!' cries Madame Barchou, 'you must take Fiona through your bedrooms first, quickly!'

51

'Oh, goody goody two shoes! But I'll need a ladder. Say, just how tall *are* you, Fiona?'

'Me first! Me first!'

'No, you'll take her in order. Fiona has now been through Rooms Eight and Nine. She must be taken in Rooms Ten Eleven Twelve Thirteen and Fourteen.'

'We'll take her! We'll take her!' they all cry in chorus. 'Fiona, we can't *wait*!'

'Shereefa is first,' announces Shereefa. 'In Room Ten we sleep on floor. Hard bed is best.'

'You know, my dear, I think Lalla Shereefa is absolutely right. I know it would be good for my back. Let's go put our mattress on the floor. Will you give me a hand, Whang?'

'This is to prepare Fiona for Antonia?'

'Well, yes.'

'And are we supposed to show her everything ... everything?'

'No, not even if you know how to do it, not *That*.'

'Not That because of the ... ah ... *physical* dangers? I didn't think Fiona had to worry about that side of things any more.'

'Standing orders are to leave That up to Antonia. After all, it's *her* trick. That's how she became a Mother Superior, after all.'

'Is it really true that Antonia has taken Holy Orders?'

'Antonia doesn't *take* orders, you know that. Antonia *gives* Holy Orders. In her own little world she's as important as the Pope. Antonia went to Japan right after the war and she bought up that ancient Shinto shrine of hers quite cheap. Restored it completely and bought up all the land around it for miles and miles around to protect the view and be utterly independent, do what she likes.'

'And we all know what *she* likes, don't we?'

'Yes, everybody has heard about Antonia's Trick ... Antonia's Trump. Ha ha, her Last Trump!'

'And you say her nuns are armed at all times?'

'No, only the Sapphic Sisters who have taken the Vow to go

armed at all times. They are the officers. Lay Lesbians are the privates. They surrender their arms every night.'

'That's a good idea,' growls Poochie. 'I don't like armed girls in my arms. I like 'em helpless . . . licked!'

'Countess Bathory,' General Whang contradicts her, 'that is *not* a good tactical idea. It is all very well for training in barracks but just think: good guerillas must never lay down their weapons and, in this man's world ours is guerilla warfare, is it not?'

'Ah, *ma générale*,' Madame Rachou placates her, 'of course you are right, but right now I suggest you all go to your rooms and prepare for Fiona while I settle some accounts before we go. Rendez-vous in the bar of the bistro.'

As we all trooped out of Madame Rachou's Room Nine, the Gurls started singing their anthem:

> VEE VEE VEE!
> YOU 'N' ME
> WE'RE THE GURLS
> OF VICTORY!
>
> YEH YEH YEH!

Shereefa took me by the hand and led me into her Room Ten which was hardly bigger than my Room Eight but it did have a window on to the narrow street below where a very noisy demonstration was going on. The Dykes on Bykes were roaring up and down on their 1000cc Triumphs and Harley Davidsons. The American squad on their gigantic old Harleys were flying the house flag of the US State Department while the British on their Triumphs carried a banner reading 'Bugger Britannia'. It was a scene right out of Burroughs but there was no use in my saying this to Shereefa even if I could talk. She wouldn't know who I was talking about anyway. And then she said, 'Just like Burroughs' book, eh? That funny old invisible man live longtime in Tangier.'

Well, you could have knocked me over with a feather and

that is just about what she did to me after pulling the curtain and stripping me. The Gurls in the hall outside and the Bykers below in the street were chanting together:

WOMEN YES
MEN NO NO
WE'RE THE SISTERS
OF SAPPHO!

YEH YEH YEH!

Shereefa took out a naked old double-edged Blue Gillette razor blade, a real relic from the early nineteenth century. Holding it delicately between middle finger and thumb, with her other tattooed fingers spread like fat little bluebirds flying around my most private parts, she shaved me. No lather. No water. No soap. It was scary, scary and a half. With no breath left to hold on to, I did my best not to twitch. I'm that sensitive. The result was quick as a flash and sensational. My whole topiary bush dropped off like a medieval merkin of matted pubic hairs used to swab out a canon. That is how we were taught to judge the value of a dictionary at Read College, by looking up to see if it had the word merkin in it or not. When Shereefa blew her keef smoke over my freshly exposed secret sexskin, I got an erection. Outside the Gurls were chanting:

YO HO HO!
'N' FIE FO FUM
TEE HEE HEE
WE'RE NOT SO DUMB

To climax however I did not come. It reminded me of that tantalizing old limerick about the young man from the Coast and the ghost, the poor ghost: 'Sighed the poor ectoplasm upon reaching her spasm, "Oh, I can feel it . . . almost".' Or it may have been Poochie's deep contralto that distracted me with the solo she was singing:

SMASH MY GLASSES
BREAK MY HEART
RIP MY GODDAM
CUNT APART!

At just that moment, Shereefa threw me across the room with a flying mare, smashing my glasses to flying splinters. Since then I have been totally blind, losing the second of my senses. However, I do think I hear better than ever and my sensual fever has been exacerbated. How I love that word! I raise my voice in song with the rest of the Gurls:

VEE VEE VEE!
VICTORY!

YOU 'N' ME
VICTORY!

When Countess Bathory picks up the song again with all that wild Hungarian Transylvanian czardas goulash in her voice, I get goose pimples all over. Shereefa is rubbing hot Moroccan spices into my delta of Venus while Poochie sings:

BITE THE BUTTON
OFF MY CLIT

YEH YEH YEH!

PUSH A HATPIN
THROUGH MY TIT

YEH YEH YEH!

It is too much, too much, too much! It is intoxicating! It is enervating! It is exacerbating and she is exacerbating me a mile a minute. Oh, what am I doing? I feel it is wildly dangerous. I may be burning up and losing forever something precious and unique. Am I a freak? It's like Shereefa and her long keef pipe with the tiny bowl that holds only one or two puffs of the precious stuff: One puff! Two puffs and *Pffft*! It's all gone forever KAPUTT!

TWIST MY ARM
SNAP MY WRIST
SMEAR MY LIPSTICK
WITH YOUR FIST . . .

Yeh yeh yeh, I say to myself weakly as I stagger out of Room Ten. When I lean against the wall to get my second wind, the door to Room Eleven opens behind me and I am drawn forcefully inside by two pairs of hands. I know immediately who it is: Gertrudnalice. They know no shame. They are pulling me, pushing me, pinching me, patting me all over with four hands. Like 'Chopsticks' on the piano. There is a lot of heavy breathing but not a word is said. Beautiful as a bird, of course, but blind as a bat am I. *Oooouuuuw! Whooooooo? Whooooo is it? Whooooo!*

SNATCH MY BUSH OUT
BY THE ROOTS
MOUNT ME WITH
YOUR COWBOY BOOTS!

I bridled. They saddled me. They rode me through the mire! Bronco busters! Bucking fucking sucking bronco busters! Whooooopeeeee! Here we *go* again. And again and again and again. Is there no end to it? When there *was* an end to it was I ever bushed, completely bushed. As soon as I staggered to my feet, four hands pushed me out into the hall but before I could pull myself together even, there opened the door to Room Twelve where Freddy and Whang were having tea.

It is all teddibly British. The duchess is pouring out of a silver teapot with a cigarette screwed into one corner of her mouth while the smoke closes her left eye in a cynical grimace. 'Sounded like the Last Roundup in there,' she snaps. 'Sit down and have a nice cup of tea, my dear. It will do you the world of good. You don't smoke, do you? I don't know why I go on smoking these ghastly cigarettes. They don't have any taste any more. Whang smokes opium or she used to. Would you like to try? Nathalie Barney is furious with me because I took Whang away from her. Not that Nathalie smoked but her buddy Violet Trefusis did and so did Madame la princesse Violette Murat although she was injecting herself with cocaine the last time I saw her. Did you ever hear the old story about her and the Bienaimée? It's really too ghastly. Delicious but ghastly, too. You see, there was this vastly wealthy picture dealer whose Bienaimée died and he had her cremated and put her ashes in an alabaster box he always had on his desk in his office or at home, I forget which. Anyway, Violet was visiting one day when he left her alone for a minute in the room. Violet loves to pry so she pried into his alabaster box in which she found this fabulous powder which she sniffed with her little platinum coke spoon she wore around her neck. Delicious, she decided before he came back. Very good stuff. So good that she found endless occasions to come back for more. It cost her a fortune because she had to buy a very expensive picture from him and find endless reasons for getting him out of the room for long enough to sniff up a good sniff. Well, not really endless, because one day the powder did come to an end. Now, this hypocritical old picture dealer had always been very hostile to addicts and swore he was not one himself but she was determined to face him with it, and, my dear, you can imagine what happened when she did. He keeled over at the idea that she had snuffed his dear dead mistress quite up.'

'Barney had a salon, a literary salon, sort of. We used to see Gertrudnalice there. We don't any more,' said Whang, 'even if they *are* just next door.'

'I'm sorry but I find them a bit of a bore,' said the duchess. 'Do you take milk in your tea, my dear? One lump or two?'

'Freddy likes something a bit rougher,' offered Whang who was fixing herself an elaborate opium pipe.

'Well, something a bit rougher than them, anyway.'

'Housemaids and country girls. Milkmaids but where to find them?'

'No, we'll leave the country girls to Erzavetta Bathory. She's run through hundreds of them in her day, cleaned out whole countrysides. In my young days, servants really still knew how to service you beginning with nannies and nursemaids who played with you in the bath, pretending to wash it for you. And then there were governesses later and saucy young housemaids with tiny waists you could get your two hot little hands around. There they were up there in their attics leaning out of tiny windows smoking forbidden cigarettes they invited you upstairs to try for the first time and some other things for the first time too, oh it was wonderful! They used to send out smoke signals when they went up in flames and they weren't very clean which was wonderful. Men are so clean they're awful. A few men were allowed at Nathalie's Friday afternoon teas but they were very old members of the French Academy who wore ear trumpets. As more and more ladies arrived, they were shunted down the long tea table until they found themselves out in the courtyard trying to seduce some pretty young pederast who'd been invited on purpose. There was always a little flock of them flitting around in the bushes or they were inside gulping down cakes and sandwiches . . .'

She talked and she chain-smoked and she chain-coughed and coughed all the time I was in there with them so that when Whang let off her extra-special Chinese fireworks for me, it was almost impossible to hear Poochie outside singing:

> VEE VEE VEE!
> PEE PEE PEE!
> YOU CAN PEE
> ALL OVER ME
> SHANGHAI SHOWERS
> HEAD TO TOE
> HONOUR ME
> SISTER SAPPHO!

Freddy and Whang led me into the chorus as we beat time with our sanitary napkins, laughing like lunatics. It was

hysterical. Are you feeling her sterical? No, she's feeling mine!
Ha ha!

> VEE VEE VEE
> YOU 'N' ME
> WE'RE THE GURLS
> OF VICTORY
>
> YEH YEH YEH!

Soon, soon, oh, all too soon! It was time to go see Elaine in
Room Thirteen and there she was slobbed out on her Jack
Daniels bourbon, alone alone alone in a big bed and quite
drunk. 'You wanna see my pussy?' she asked me, slyly offering to turn down the covers. She had a Coca Cola bottle down
there in her. That was enough for me. I didn't need to learn
that lesson, thank you very much but no thanks. I'd heard
about girls having to have Coke bottles taken out, surgically.
'G'wan over an' see Poochie,' she offered. 'Poochie's got the
real thing. She'll show ya.'

I did and she did and it was all I could do to get out of there
alive, if that's what you call it. I can't say that just to think of it
makes my blood run cold because my blood doesn't even run
any more. Poochie proved that for me. Try as she might, she
could not get one more drop of blood out of me.

I reeled out of Room Fourteen, the last on that second floor,
to slide down the stairs into the warm arms of Lalla Shereefa
who was waiting for me just outside the bathroom into which
she took me and washed me. It all happened so quickly.
Whooosht! I must have slipped on some of my own old business, I guess. Yes, Shereefa taught me how to wash myself
properly, beginning with the fingers and toes, working
upwards and inwards until one's whole skin rolls off the
whole body. It was like being born again, spotless. Then she
wound me into a sheet with one titty hanging out like Diana
the Huntress and steered me down the front hall to the bistro
where everyone was waiting for me.

There was a noisy demonstration going on out in the street. Appalling conditions were breaking loose out there in Shit-in-the-Bed Street. The narrow alley was roaring with a wild pack of savage Dykes on Bykes as big as dinosaurs, so they told me. Unnatural forces taking over. Gigantic Gurls in leather and chains are tearing up and down on their Yamahas and their Kawasakis and Suzukis. Gurls are rapping on the windows of the bistro with mailed fists but Madame Rachou will not let them in.

'No no no!' she cries. 'Quick quick quick! Help me pull up this heavy trapdoor in the floor. This is how we get big barrels of wine up and down from the cellars. There now, you see! Here it comes. Just jump on to this little hydraulic platform and away we go to Antonia's party!'

'Are you sure this contraption will hold us?'

'Oooh, there's nothing to hold on to!'

'Hold on to me. Hold on to me. Hold on to *me*!'

'Will you just shine that electric torch down there to let me see how deep it is?'

'You mean a flashlight, doncha?'

'I don't think this thing's safe, do you?'

'You have to be kidding. This looks like a rabbit-hole.'

'Say, Fiona, how much do you weigh anyway?'

'*Allons, mes enfants! Allons allons!*' Madame Rachou cries above the unholy din from the street. '*Allons, mes filles!* Ladies ladies! Down we go! Quickly quickly!' She is clapping her hands as sharp as pistol shots.

'*Geroooooonimo!*'

'Down the hatch!'

'Does that French mother know what she's sayin'? Downa hatch means you toss off a drink.'

'Toss off?'

'Oh, up your giggy with a wire brush, you!'

'What kinda talk is that from a lady.'

My ears were popping. The air was whistling past my ears. My ears were popping. I thought we were going on down for-ever and then we stopped with a jolt and a bump and a bounce that threw us all off the little platform. The stone floor was slippery and it seemed to be raining, drizzling, dripping.

'Put on your sou'westers!' screamed Madame Rachou. 'Here, turn that light on the water. Don't fall in there. That's the river, our little underground river, La Chie. You know what that means, don't you? Don't drink a drop of it or you'll forget what you ever knew, who you are and where you are going and everything.'

'Just where *are* we going?'

'We are going to Antonia's Annual Party. There will be an unmanned skiff coming along here in a minute or two and we must try to catch the very first one because they only come by at critical intervals. We mustn't be late for the party.'

'My paws and whiskers,' chuckled the duchess, 'it's a pity you didn't bring your kayak, Fiona, but we couldn't all fit into it, could we?'

'Does anyone here know how to handle a boathook?'

'It's a pity you can't see all this, Fiona, because it's really rather wonderful in an eerie sort of way, like Piranesi's imaginary prisons or the Carlsbad Caverns or my grandfather's gold mines in Montana. Why is that water so black and so oily, Madame Rachou?'

'Because that oily black swift-flowing surface is ink, printers' ink, as you will see in a minute. Ah, here comes our unmanned skiff on the current. Be quick with that boathook and catch it. There, that was clever. We've got it. Now, hold on to its painter because the current is very swift and strong. Put on your hard hats, girls. Man the boat.'

'Woman the boat, doncha mean? OK, Fiona, you're first.'

'But Fiona's the heaviest.'

'That's why. We'll see if the skiff can take her. Look, the water is already almost up to the gunwales.'

'Don't be silly, get in everybody! Just get in one at a time and sit down without rocking the boat.'

'Is everybody aboard? Cast off!'

'I can't see a thing, not one fucking thing,' Shereefa complains.

'Neither can I,' I laugh.

But I, curiously enough, I could. I could see, sort of. I who could see nothing else, could see in the dark or I thought I could. There was nothing to see. We seemed to be speeding down a swiftly flowing channel between greasy black banks. The low arched vault overhead made it more like a tunnel. It was dripping water everywhere.

'You know,' the duchess was saying in a dreamy voice in my ear, 'this reminds me of something, but what is it? Is it a sort of sideshow, an attraction they used to have in the old Luna Park here in Paris, or was it in a fairground I was taken to by my governess? Oh when, oh where? Above ground, they had these rather sickening things like the Ferris Wheel and the Roller Coaster. I didn't really like that. What I liked were the more secretive pleasures like these mysterious rides through the dark in a skiff on swift-flowing water. They called it The Tunnel of Love, I remember. You bought a ticket to get into a flat-bottomed boat, an unmanned skiff just like this, and you were off on the current. First, a man took your ticket . . . like Marriage . . . Romance, I suppose. You paid. Or your parents paid. That was the Contract. And then you took off. You took off in the dark, of course. That was part of the price you paid. You were frightened, scared stiff but excited. At least I was. Weren't *you*, my dear Whang?'

'No. I never was married. I was drafted. If I hadn't been drafted I would have been killed. Exposed on a mountainside. Girls were not of much value in China. My mother made only girls. I was the last out of eight. In the famine year, they sold me to the Warlord as a very cheap boy. I thought I was too, and so did everyone else. I had all the girls I wanted. No one complained. I advanced through the ranks. I was decorated. I became an officer. I was decorated many times more. After a great victory in Outer Mongolia, I was summoned to the Summer Palace. The Dowager Empress received me. She made me a general.'

'For a great victory over her enemies?'

'No, for kissing the Lotus. The Sacred Stem of the Lotus, it was called.'

'Kissing the Lotus, the Sacred Stem of the Lotus! Oh Whang, how *very* exciting. You never told me all this before. What was it like? Tell me.'

'Pretty big, considering, the Stem of it was.'

'How big?'

'As big as the sex on a man. I mean a Chinaman, of course.'

'Her Imperial Clitoris!'

'Yes. It was no time to turn tail.'

'You mean she would have buggered you?' broke in Elaine.

'She would have cut off my head.'

'She would have done it herself?' suggested Poochie eagerly.

'No, some palace eunuch would have complied only too readily. Two high-ranking eunuchs were there to part her heavily embroidered brocade skirt in front of me as I made my obeisance, striking the ground between her tiny bound feet with my forehead. When I raised my eyes, the lips of her vulva were being delicately parted by two eunuchs with jade chopsticks. The Stem of the Lotus protruded. I approached it very reverentially with the tip of my tongue. She reached around my head with the 12-inch long fingernails of her left hand and . . .'

'And then? Oh do go on, Whang, I'm getting excited!'

'Stop rocking the boat! We're shipping water. Don't anyone move!'

'Yeah. Don't nobody make no fool moves, see.'

'Ms Waterbee, you the one's rocking this boat,' says Shereefa as she pulls out her Zippo lighter to light the long slim keef pipe she draws out of her sleeve. She takes two or three deep drags on the pipe and then very adroitly spits out the blazing red coal which zips through the air like a comet to sizzle out in the black water of the Chie.

'Say, that smells like great grass, Shereefa. D'ja bring it with ya from Morocco? Where can I score for some of that?'

'*Eeek!*' screeches the duchess, 'have we got addicts aboard?'

We began to see visions, all of us. There were sparkling

lights ahead and as we came around the corner, Freddy breathed, 'It's the Place de la Concorde or the Place Louis Quinze, you can't quite tell which because there's a little of both of them. Look up there on that balcony and you see that family of American tourists, that's me and my family when I was a little girl and first came to Paris. We stayed in the Hôtel Crillon there and they hadn't yet built the new American Embassy right next door on the left where you see that eighteenth-century house dating back to before the French Revolution or the American one. Why, there is no obelisk yet in the centre of the place, is there? And there, there, right there! Look, there is the guillotine and some young lady is having her head cut off by the executioner. Do you all see what I see? He is holding her head up for everyone to see. How dreadful, and how is it that we are watching it? Nothing moves. It must be a waxwork.'

'I think it's just a Deceptual Art Show. I've seen things at the Museum just like that. Events. Art Events. I think that head belongs to Mate Killit the deceptual sculptress.'

'My dear Fiona!' cried Gertrudnalice in one voice as one woman, 'it's just as well you cannot see these horrors. Mate Killit deserved it, but the new old *tableau vivant* or whatever it is we have in front of us now is really too utterly revolting for words!'

'Don't put it in words, then, I pray you,' mocked the duchess. 'Fiona, what we are looking at is really just too appalling. I simply cannot tell you how truly appalling it is.'

'Well, don't tell her then,' insisted Elaine. 'I simply hate violence!'

'I've seen worse things in war,' opined General Whang.

'I've seen worse things than that in my own castle in Outer Transylvania. In the bathroom,' snickered Countess Bathory.

'Erzavetta Bathory, you should be banished from decent society.'

'I was until the Americans came along and reinstated me.'

'You should have been walled up forever in that infamous bathroom of yours.'

'I was. For 227 years, two months and four days until my good friends in the United States Department sent the OSS to free me, I was walled up in there.'

'Why Poochie, you never told me all this. How *did* you get along? Howdja eat frinstance?'

'Oh, peasant girls kept coming up in baskets.'

'You mean, coming up *with* baskets, don't you?'

'No, I let down a basket on a long rope and drew them up into the castle.'

'Why didn't you escape, then, with that same basket?'

'Oh, you couldn't get down again. The rope wasn't long enough.'

'But Poochie, I don't see how . . .'

'You may not choose to see, Mrs Waterbee,' the duchess chimed in, 'but we do. Perfectly.'

'I knew those two girls by sight,' said Madame Rachou, dreamily, 'saw them in church on Sundays with that old couple who cared for them, took them in out of the orphanage. They worked the farm next to ours and that big girl did all the heavy work. Her younger sister was not quite right in the head and she always defended her. The old man caught the younger one smoking in the barn and beat her with a pitchfork before he locked her up in the root cellar. The big girl, there, came in off the fields on her tractor and grabbed an axe to chop the door down and let out her sister. Then they charged into the kitchen where the old couple were having their dinner and chopped them to pieces. Jean Genet wrote a play about them and even before him the Surrealists made socialist heroines of them, the Papin Sisters.'

'My dear Madame Rachou,' insisted the duchess, 'those are not the Soeurs Papin. Look, you can see it's not a French kitchen but an American one. That big girl is Lizzie Borden from Fall River, Mass. near where *I* was born in New England. She's a legend. A Fall River legend. There's a Jerome Robbins ballet about her and New England kids still sing a nursery rhyme about her, or they did in *my* childhood:

Lizzie Borden took an axe
To give her father forty whacks
When she saw what she had done
She gave her mother forty-one!

Her mother or her father, I forget which came first, but she did it to both of them. I don't know how she got off. Glad I never had any children. The duke wasn't up to it, thank God. Vicious little beasts. But Lizzie became quite the national heroine.'

'*Je n'insiste pas*,' Madame Rachou insists with a narrow smile, 'but those are les Soeurs Papin. I'd know them any day.'

'Lizzie Borden! Lizzie Borden!' screams Freddy.

'Yes,' said Gertrudnalice as one woman, 'we spent a summer with her in Fall River when she was quite old. We read the Greek tragedies aloud every night. She took the part of Clytemnestra. You know: *This house smells of blood* and all that. It did, too.'

It was getting colder and colder.

'Say, I'm freezing. Howzabout you? Hey, is that ice I see on the water? What are we coming to, Siberia? What river is this, anyway, the Volga? You know, my folks came over from Russia. This looks familiar. You hear that howling? That's wolves. Or it's a recording. No, look, there! Real live wolves or is it a holograph of them? No, look, they're digging up corpses out of the snow and eating them. It looks as if there's been a battle here recently. And there they are, the Red Guards with their prisoners, all those raggedy soldiers all bundled up. Over there where that little fire is, those are their officers. They've surrendered. They've had to empty out all their pockets and hand over their sable-lined winter pelisses to the Red Guards, those burly ones there with the red star on their cloth caps. They're going through and dividing up all that jewellery, all that genuine Fabergé they stripped off the officers.

Diamonds glittering in the snow! Ice on ice! Cigarette cases and cigarette holders of platinum utterly encrusted with diamonds, jewelled crosses and holy medals along with the military ones, signet rings and slave bracelets along with a whole nest of diamond-studded Easter eggs. Oh, the Red Guards are forming a firing squad and frog-marching someone across the blood-stained snow to the stake. Why, that's too awful! It's a woman. Look, she has just dropped her sables and she's wearing nothing but her beautiful long auburn hair blowing across her beautiful bare breasts. They can't shoot *her*. I won't let them. Hey, stop that, youse guys. Cut it out! Ixnay! You know why? Because I'm that woman. That's *me* over there and those are *my* sables and *my* red hair!'

'Your red hair? You mean all this is happening before you bought that red rug you wear on your head?'

'I'm an orthodox married woman and I should wear a shadel.'

'Besides, she caught typhoid in Tiflis,' offered her pal Poochie.

'You mean thyroid from syphilis.'

'*Mesdames! Mesdames!*' cries Madame Rachou, 'Ladies! Ladies! *Un peu de retenu, s'il vous plaît!* I don't know how to translate that.'

'Decency. The word decency will do.'

'Before the revolution, my father made us all sable coats down to the ground. I've got pictures of us dripping with sables.'

'A fur Jew's daughter,' sneers Lalla Shereefa. 'In Morocco we don't have fur coats. Too hot.'

'Why, who the devil is that oriental-looking officer commanding the firing squad? Is that you, Whang?' demands Freddy fiercely. 'It looks just like you. Who *are* you, Whang? And what side are you on, really? Are you really a bloody Bolshie? Tell me, Whang, tell me!'

'That's not me,' replies Whang unperturbed. 'You know we all look alike, us orientals.'

'No, no,' Madame Rachou reassures Freddy, 'that's not

your Whang. Maybe another one, maybe. They all *do* look alike, you know, *vraiment*.'

'Not to me,' cries the duchess bravely.

'Poochie,' orders Elaine, 'sing *Black Eyes*, you know, our version.'

Erzavetta Bathory sings in a deep contralto like sour cream stirred into magenta-coloured bortsch:

> *Oh tchin tchornyia*
> *Oh tchin skrasnyia*
> *Scratch my assnyia*
> *Make a passnyia*
> *I'll bust ya snatchnyia . . .*

'Shut up!' screams the duchess. 'We have young ears around here. Think of Fiona.'

'I think about Fiona all day and all night. I can't help it. She's in my blood.'

'You mean her last drop of blood is in you, you vile vampire. Thank God we're not going to be exposed to a *tableau vivant* of any of *your* past activities in Outer Transylvania.'

'Don't you say nothin' bad about my Poochie or you'll find out!'

'If she goes on singing that brand of, well, marmalade, frankly, I'll see to it that she never gets to Antonia's party alive.'

'So, who's alive any more? Take it easy, duchess, we're all in the same boat.'

'You're right. You're absolutely right. Let's sing something lively, some cowgirl songs like: *She Swore that She Loved Her but Oh How She Lied*! You remember the rest of the words? How does it go? *She Tore Down Her Panties Just Fit to be Tied*? Like that, hmmmm? No?'

'No, it goes: *She Never Could Make Her but Oh How She Tried*!'

'Oh, how vulgar, how . . . how *paltry* all this is! I wish this skiff would sink, don't you? Suddenly sink under us and take us all to the bottom, hmmm?'

'No, frankly . . . no, I don't. Just fill your ears with what Poochie is going to sing. It's an enchanting czardas from her native heath in Transylvania.'

Poochie sings, in a deep oily baritone:

> *As I loll*
> *Upon the Lethe*
> *I can feel it roll*
> *Beneath me . . .*
> *I'm coming!*
> *Yes, I'm coming!*
> *I'm coming*
> *On its tide!*
>
> *O K, Chairon,*
> *Keep your hair on.*
> *I'll pay you*
> *With my hide!*
> *I know you*
> *Can't be bought.*
> *Here's a penny*
> *For your thoughts.*
>
> *It's to pay you*
> *For the ride!*

'Mmmmm!' murmured the duchess in apparent appreciation, 'a most beee*youuu*tiful song! And how apt, in our present situation. *But*, my dear, I'm not quite clear about your classical references. Wasn't Charon the boatman on the Styx? Didn't one pay one's obole . . . one's penny . . . to him? Hmm? And that was to get *into* Hades, I believe. While the Lethe was the river whose water one drank to for*get* one's previous incarnation. On the way back *out* of Hades. Correct me if I am wrong! But that is all so *far*, far away that almost no one gets her classical references right any more, does she?'

'Pick pick pick!' snorts Elaine. 'You give me a pain duchess, with your nit-picking. Poochie knows what she's talking about. Y'know. I made it with Poochie for *years* before I really and truly realized just how deep she is. She was so deep into the, uh . . . well, uh . . . mystery of it. Of *love*, I mean . . . that she would never let me turn on the lights at night even. Y'unnerstand me? The first time she would let me turn on the lights, it was in a real fleabag hotel in Marseilles. Poochie said it was to scare the cockroaches away. Was I ever disgusted! It was all her idea and was I ever scared. I've got this fear of flying so there we were taking the night train from Paris and a boat to Tangier where all those *Ay*rabs were waiting for poor little Yiddische me. I simply could not imagine why Poochie wanted to go there so bad. But I guess she heard about all them harem-scarems and deep massage in the steam baths – the hammams – so she just had to go there to find out for herself. And for *me* too, so help me. Well, it's true, let me tell you, it's terrific. In those hammams we ran into some femmes who tipped two hunnert, three hunnert, *four* hunnert pounds soakin' wet on the steamroom scales. And were they ever heavy chicks, let me tell you. It didn't take a whole lot to get them goin' and when they went, they went on for*ever*! I mean they juss coudden *stop*! It was *crazy. Real* crazy! First thing, one of these chicks whips out an old-fashioned straight razor . . . a cut-throat . . . an' shaves off her delta of Venus right there on the hot marble floor in front of everybody. Was I ever embarrassed . . . *scared*, even. And as for that intimate massage. I wanna tellya! It was downright unbelievable. One skinny old chick with muscles like whipcord was tying a plump young chick into *knots*! In all the dark corners, were there *ever* . . . uh well, uh . . . situations. *Things* goin' on! My own old Jewish mother would never have believed that femmes could get into positions like that. But then my momma was arthritic all of her life. You know, you simply coudden believe your own *eyes*. What you saw happenin' down there.'

'Perhaps your glasses fogged over,' offered Freddy charitably. 'Or were you not wearing your contacts at the time?'

'You think I'm drunk, doncha? Well, I'm drunk on my old memories. I know it's all over. Everything. But lemme tell ya, in a spot like that hammam you hadda keep a clear head. Some of these chicks come up on ya in the old dressing room afterwards, makin' ta . . . well, uh . . . ta pick up some quick change. Ya gotta be firm with 'em. Believe me, sayin': Look here sweetie, if ya really think about it, *I* pleasured *you*! How's *about 'at*, chicken? *I'm* the one that oughtta get paid. Not you.'

'Yes. I know what you mean,' Freddy admitted ruefully. 'I guess we've all been through that sort of thing. Haven't we?'

'Not me,' said la Bathory, alias Poochie. 'Of course, sometimes, I've had to pay, uh, compensation to the families. To the girl's *families*, you know. Afterwards. When I couldn't give the girls back, because they were in such poor condition or not quite . . . how shall I say? . . . complete.'

'Poochie is the soul of honesty. I'd trust her with my last nickel. She's punctilious! That's what she is.'

'Nothing like that ever happened to me,' Whang assured Freddy. 'I would have put them up in front of a firing squad or decapitated them myself.'

'Well, that's all very well for the two of you to say but there was a war goin' on at the time with Israel and we found ourselves about two hunnert feet *unner*ground, like in a *mine*. We were told that these hot baths were discovered first by the Romans who carved out this loong looong flight of greasy steps going doown and dooown without banisters. Only a rope to hang on to. And was I ever scared. Poochie was fearless and helped me to hold on to the slippery rope. As we skidded down this last flight of stone steps we fell into a heap of truly enormously fat Ayrab ladies who were whacking each other with big wooden paddles. And the *noise* that it made was like *gun*fire echoing back and forth throughout these underground galleries, the old Roman bath. The hot rooms were as big as chapels in a cathedral. Lit only by a candle or two. And the *gurls* were really taking *care* of each other in dark *cor*ners with *in*timate *deep* mas*sage*.'

'You remember that girl in the hottest room of them all? What she could do with her toes?'

'Well . . . I was pretty relaxed and enjoying it until I realized that she didn't have any hands. Leprosy was the first thought that flashed through my mind.'

71

'Oh, I know that girl,' grunted Shereefa, spitting the red coal out of her keef pipe to sizzle into the murky waters of the Chie. 'She one bad thief. One big thief. She steal too much, they cut her off two hand. Then they cut her off two foots. She even steal one foots. Bad, bad. She take one big thing off ya?'

'Oh! Noooo,' breathed Elaine. 'It was all just so *beau*tiful! Quite the *best* deep massage I almost ever *had* except for things that are ... well ... sacred between Poochie and *me*, of course. No, the poor girl wouldn't take *any*thing. She wouldn't even accept a little something I offered her.'

'Some sing how little?'

'How do you mean, how little? I put it down on the ground in front of her. She didn't have any hands, after all.'

'She just leave it lay there, eh?'

'Why yes. I was deeply touched.'

'Touch again ... not 'nuff.'

'Oh, how can you say that? I think she ... well ... *loved* me. You know what I mean? Or don't they *have* that in your country?'

'Not without money. Not in Morocco. In Algeria, maybe.'

'You're from Morocco, aren't you? What do you *do* there? ... what *did* you do?'

'I don't hafta do nuttin. I'm a saint. A hereditary saint.'

'How ab-so-*lute*ly *fas*cinating! What do saints do? I've always wondered.'

'Oh, go 'round 'n' round. Give blessings. Get gifts. Pick up holy taxes. That thing like that. I give one hand for kiss. You wanna touch?'

'You mean I should cross your palm with something?'

'No no. Juss touch. Put it anywhere. It's worth sumpin. Put it between your thighs.'

'Oh no, I don't think I could afford that.'

'No go ahead. Try your luck. You may be lucky one.'

'Oh, go ahead, Elaine. Don't always be thinking about your money. It really doesn't mean anything any more at this point in the trip.'

'Well, if Poochie doesn't mind, but ... just tell me one thing, what am I going to get out of it?'

'An orgasm. Maybe.'

'You *must* be kidding.'

'Well *try!*'

'I won't have anyone rocking this skiff and I mean it!' snaps Madame Barchou with authority. 'No orgasms on board until we get to Antonia's landing.'

'Everything is permitted at this point,' insists the duchess. 'Nothing is forbidden any more.'

'Except bad manners, Confucius say.'

'Oh well, you're quite right, my dear Whang. I was forgetting myself, I stand corrected. What I really wanted to say was that ... you'll remember, we had a mutual friend in Morocco ... in Marrakesh, who had the most unfortunate adventure. She was taken ... *very* taken with a young thing of not very robust constitution who ... ah, *died* on her, if I may be permitted to use that term. Our friend was from one of the very best families, I won't mention her name, Lalla Shereefa, in case you might know them, you most certainly *do*, but, well, our perhaps mutual friend was a *very* hard taskmistress. Very demanding. Of a most passionate nature, she *gave* and she expected in return ... quite a lot. This girl, now, from a great feudal family in the Atlas mountains wasn't up to it. Not quite. An accident occurred. Our friend had been here in Paris where we introduced her to Antonia. And ... in the natural course of things ... she learned, or was taught, Antonia's Trick, as it's come to be called: the Last Trump. *She* survived it. She not only survived it but she took it back to Morocco with her as part of her stock in trade ... if I might *call* it that. As I said, the girl died, died in orgasm, I believe. Shereefa, our friend, a*noth*er Shereefa that is, not this Lalla Shereefa here, was disconsolate. She wept and she wept and she wept. She felt that life was no longer worth living without her young friend. She felt that she could not go on living without her fair form, nightly, in her embrace. I don't know who it was gave her the idea but she decided to have her friend stuffed, flayed

73

and stuffed. It's quite simple to have someone flayed while they're living, as you must know, Countess Bathory, you've had it done often enough. But if you do it after death a certain amount of resilience is lost. Is it not so?'

'Yes yes. Oh yes yes. Yes yes.'

'So ... our friend took a double-edged Blue Gillette razor blade to remove her friend's *hide*.'

'*Skin*, you mean.'

'No no. I mean *hide*. Skin is just this superficial covering we all have to keep our blood inside, while our *hide* is as tough as shoeleather when you tan it. Seven layers thick, as you know. It makes very fine lampshades, cigarette cases ... uh, a young American composer friend of ours, Jill's gay husband Jack as a matter of fact, found this out when he had the left breast ... or should I say the chest? of a friend of his uncle's, made into a cigarette case, whose, ah, nipple one pressed to get out a smoke.'

'You hafta be kiddin'!'

'No no. I'm not! It was a beautiful object, with golden blond hairs, the man was a *Swede* I believe. Some local boy he picked up stole it from him, in Mexico. Filthy place. So utterly corrupt. Well. What was I talking about?'

'About this girl in Marrakesh whose ladyfriend died on her.'

'Oh yes. She had her hide tanned and stuffed.'

'Now you *haf*ta be kidding!'

'I swear I am not. She simply could not get to sleep without her, you see. So she had her flayed, as I said, with a double-edged Blue Gillette razor blade held between thumb and middle finger ...'

'Oh mi*gawd*! That's what might've happened to *me* in that hammam, those baths, them *Ay*rabs!'

'And *then*?'

'And then she sent the hide out to the tanners, on the outskirts of the city of Marrakesh. You know how that place smells!'

'Ooh! Do I not! I mean do I ever! Ugh!'

'Yes. They use human faeces and urine to tan the leather.

74

That's what gets it so soft. Filthy people those tanners. They went to the police about it. And *all* our friend *want*ed was to have the girl stuffed in order to fuck her, that is, to keep herself warm in winter. You know how cold and wet it can get there in Marrakesh in wintertime.'

'And what happened then?'

'Nothing much. Lalla Shereefa just got twenty years to *life*, that's all, at *hard* labour. As we all know, human justice is still in the hands of male chauvinist *pigs*!'

'Say, my feet are getting wet! Either we're shipping water or this skiff has sprung a leak. Shereefa, would you give us a little light here with your Zippo? There, you see, there's six inches of water in here. We've got to bail her out. Who's got something to bail us out with? Maybe one of Fiona's boots. Take off your boots, Fiona. Ooops! Be careful, Fiona, we've just shipped a whole lot more water. Look, Madame Barchou, look look look! This water has letters in it. It's thick with letters like alphabet soup.'

'*C'est la Chie*,' Madame Barchou replies, calmly turning her miner's lamp on the bottom of the boat, first, and then sweeping the surrounding waters with it. '*C'est comme ça*. It's been polluted like that ever since the beginning of printing. Pollution. Word pollution. Logorrhoea. You see, the publishing houses are further upstream on the shady side of our street and when they can't sell a book, why, they pulp it and pour it back into the Chie.'

'What a waste.'

'Oh, it's only the words that are wasted and washed away down the drains. The pulped paper is salvaged and bleached of the inky words which are wrung out when this . . . this porridge is pressed out and rolled into reams of paper again to be reprinted with words. So it goes on. Nothing is lost but the worthless words which pour through here on their way to the river beneath Antonia's windows and then on down to the sea, I suppose,' she finished dreamily. 'The Sea!'

'*Nuestras vidas son rios, que van a dar en la mar!*' sings Poochie deliciously.

'So don't tell me words are worthless!' cried the duchess. 'I've used lots of words in a lifetime and I know what they're worth. Of course, there are all *sorts* of words, aren't there, and some are worth more than others. Some people's word may be worthless and words may be worth more at one time than at another but look down there, look! The waters of the Chie are phosphorescent with the exquisite deliquescence of decaying words . . .'

'I do.'

'What do you mean, Ms Waterbee?'

'I mean that every time I said I do at the altar or in front of the judge or at the registrar's office, it meant a whole lot more bread for me. I've been married a lot.'

'Oh yes, but that isn't what I was talking about, I . . .'

'Sidi Sherkh al-Alawi,' Shereefa pronounced flatly, 'say: *El Ahl Dyal Kiz*! . . .!' she went on in Arabic.

'I don't understand a word of Arabic, what does that mean?'

'He say: *The Soul of Words is in the Ink*.'

'That sounds pretty profound. Just let me think about it for a minute . . .'

'No Ink, no Letter. No Letter, no Word. No Word, no Book.'

'I'll go along with that. It sound perfectly reasonable. Not all that profound, perhaps. You see, Shereefa, what we're talking about is bad books.'

'There is no bad books,' Shereefa insisted stoutly. 'The Books is sacred!'

'Oh, of course, Shereefa, *THE Book* is sacred but we are talking about books the publisher can't get rid of. They can't sell them or even remainder them in the bookstalls down by the Seine. They can't give them away. Nobody wants them even as a gift. They can't burn them. That is forbidden. It is absolutely forbidden to burn books. They used to burn books and their publishers along with them like poor Etienne Dolet over there in the Place Maubert. He was not only burned at the stake in the 1500s but even his bronze statue was knocked down by the Nazis here in the 1940s to burn him a second time, melted him down to make cannons. That sort of thing got a very bad name, so they boil them.'

'Thay fwhat? Boil publishers?'

'No, they boil books, boil them in vats with a bleacher in the water to leach out the words, the ink.'

'Is better?' asked Shereefa, utterly shocked. 'Boil them? That hurts.'

'Look,' said Madame Rachou with a little laugh, 'just look into this inky black water by the light of my lamp. It looks perfectly black out there, doesn't it, black as ink? But here in my hand when I cup some up ... not that I'd drink it, *parbleu*! ... but you can see that the colour is pure illusion and so are the letters unless they have been anointed with ink.'

'No,' states la Bathory flatly, 'not true. I just picked up a very bad word in Hungarian, look!'

'Well, nobody here but you reads Hungarian, my dear. Are you sure it isn't just a piece of pied type? All the words in the world must be flowing through here. Hush! If you'd all just stop talking for a minute, perhaps we could make out what they are saying as they babble, bubble ... mutter, mumble ... murmuring old slogans, old saws ... all human memory ... a palimpsest ...'

'*L'immense et compliqué palimpseste de la mémoire*,' murmurs Madame Rachou. 'M'sieu Baudelaire said that. He used to drop into my bistro for a glass of wormwood with Gérard de Nerval, as he called himself, and that nice little M'sieu Latouche: he was so witty we all laughed, even M'sieu Baudelaire. He didn't laugh much. He lived with his mother. She and her second husband, le Général Aupic, lived just up the street and across the square. He had to go home to lunch alone with her every single day in the week and he was often drunk by then. He was morbid and surly when he was drunk. I liked him a lot. He always looked to me like someone who'd been a long time in jail. He had that look. He kept a permanent room in the hotel to do his writing in.'

'*Les Fleurs du Mal*?'

'No, *Le Festin Nu*. The police came here and took away all

the copies to pulp them and pour them into the Chie right under our street, under our feet and under his nose. He used to sit there in my bistro morosely preparing his absinthe, letting the water drip drop by drop through a lump of sugar, turning it cloudy as one of his black moods would settle down on him and he would turn nasty, poor man. He always said the water was washing away his words and like that nice young English tubercular poet he admired so much who died in Rome, his name was writ in water, *le pauvre.*'

'But no!' cried the duchess. 'His words are immortal. I'm sure even Fiona here knows them: *Lesbos, où les baisers sont comme les cascades!*'

I merely hung my head and went on bailing out the boat. I'd never even heard of this Baudelaire but the word Lesbos made me prick up my ears. I thought I knew what they were talking about and it made me blush.

Freddy laughed. 'Well, if you can still blush, Fiona, that's a good sign. Your heart's still in the right place. His best poems are about love between women and I know them all by heart. We learned them in French class with the nuns at the Convent of the Sacred Heart. That was a long time ago. The nightingales were singing there. That's where I got my start. My, aren't we taking a hell of a long time getting nowhere, hmm? You know what I mean. When do we get to Antonia's landing? What's holding us up, hmm?'

Alone, utterly alone in the dark. Where did they go? Up, I guess. There was a lot of talk about me being too big, as usual. They went up one by one because this French elevator . . . this contraption, as they called it, was too fragile. Elaine said it looked like a birdcage bouncing up and down on twisted rubber bands and she carried on a lot before she would get into it without her Poochie. When they had all gone up without me, she was the only one brave enough to come back and encourage me. I was standing there in a puddle of water from the Chie. I could feel the filthy old words from failed books crawling up my legs.

'You Whooo! You who, Fiona!' called Elaine from a distance somewhere overhead. 'I'm coming, oh, shit shit shit! There I go, I've pressed the wrong button again. These Parisian elevators, aren't they something else! You wanna know how this one works? You push this button here and what does it do? It gooses a spider. I mean it, it gooses a real genuine giant Black Widow spider Antonia keeps up in the attic of this fantastic house of hers she has up there and you know what she does? The Black Widow spider, I mean. She loosens the cable she spins out or she sucks it all back up again and ... Oh, shit shit shit! I pushed that other wrong button so now I'll be leaving you before I even got down there to see you. This birdcage, as I call it, hangs on the thread this trained spider of hers ... Don't despair. Help is coming. I just wanna tell ya, babe, there's one hell of a party going on up here ...'

Alone again, utterly alone in the dark. What to do? What to do now? Call on my guru, of course. Why haven't I thought of her before? I call her. She comes. I take a cool critical look at her as she taught me to do. She always said: Beware of imitations. As it is, she is looking just a little bit too, well, too oriental today. A little too Kwanyin, if you know what I mean. She's overdoing the motherly look. The end result is that you see her soft firmness is a cover for cruelty. Her cool smile is all kindness, all understanding but when you look closer you see that placid stupidity overlies evident cunning. I don't like the look of that fat brocade cushion she is sitting crosslegged on in the lotus position and I don't like the look of that little curlicue cloud hanging behind her head with a halo in it. These props belong in a cheap bazaar. My eye for oriental art was museum-trained. How come I had never noticed this before? Have I been taken in? Is my guru a fake?

She gives me the nod. This is an imperious imperial gesture bidding me join her on her rug, not to share her chintzy cushion beside her but just sit on the very edge of her rug. I climb on to it clumsily and we go up and up and up.

When we get there, is it ever noisy, noisy as hell! It sounds like a riot at a rock concert runover by a clash between the Hags and the Fags. Through all this I hear Freddy shrieking, 'Ah, there you are, Fiona my dear. I've been looking everywhere for you. I sent word to Antonia saying you were too big to get into that ridiculous little lift of hers ... it doesn't deserve to be called an elevator ... and she sent back word saying she was taking care of it. Antonia is always as good as her word. Now, come along and I'll introduce you to everybody who is anybody from Zee to A. This is Queen Zenobia of Palmyra. Watch out for Her Majesty, she's had one or two bourbons too many. Zenobia will excuse us if we move on. She should sign up with AA. I have the printed list here but there are a great many more ladies than that here present tonight: Yolanda, that must be Yolanda of Montenegro, you'd like her, she's just about your size. Six eight. Couldn't play basketball, though. Queen of Italy. Here's Xenia, she couldn't either because she has a peg leg, the left leg if I remember correctly. She calls herself a Serene Highness. One of the most neurotic women I ever knew. You wouldn't want her on your team, either. She's tough, though. Used to beat up that effeminate husband of hers. Somebody wrote an opera about them. A funny marriage. No funnier than mine, though. Where was I? What letter? I think it's plain silly to list Christina of Sweden under Q for Queen, don't you, hmm? Don't think she's coming. Too busy elsewhere. Thinks she's got it made, like Sappho.

'Let's see: Lily Marlene, who's she? Elsa Maxwell over there gave huge parties, never cost her a cent. Don't know how she did it. Let's ask her. Lady Elsie Mandly, that's a mistake. Esther Chester Arthur, she was mad, mad about Madame de Pompadour, claimed Nancy Mitford scooped her there. No wonder. She has a wall-eye like Sartre. It made one quite dizzy to see them together. Dalkusha de Rohan, lovely name, lovely lady. Mercedes d'Acosta, Garbo's pal. Bigfoot. Elizabetta instead of Erzavetta Bathory. This list doesn't make any sense but I'll introduce you to all of them. Hold on, here's the letter O. O for Orla the Transextite, she's made Antonia's list at last.

And there's Katinka Klein from Kansas City with Nazimova and Natasha Rambova and all those other Glammer Gurls from Hollywood before and since. Ah, Colette is talking with the British Bunch of literary ladies, Virginia Woolf and Vita Sackville-West and there's our Janie, surrounded by the Gurls' Gang from New York: *Vogue, Harper's Bazaar, Time* and *Life* and *Fortune*, the whole Research Department. Where's Helvetia? Here, it says: Jane and Shereefa. Not our Shereefa but the other one Janie picked up in Tangier. There are lots of Shereefas but that one isn't a descendant of the Prophet. Can't be, since she's a Berber. One can't be too careful about that sort of thing. It's like all those phony marquises in France. Thank God my duke was a real duke. They always are. They have to be, they cost enough. There are NO phony dukes. Dukes stick together. My Dear Departed called them his Fellow Workers. Very hard work.'

> VEE VEE VEE
> YOU 'N' ME
> WE'RE THE GURLS
> OF VICTORY!

'My dear, there's so much noise in there I can hardly hear myself speak!'

'Oh, c'mon Freddy! Join the conga line!'

'A conga line! Do you Gurls realize where we are? We're in the private chapel of Joan of Arc! I don't think Antonia would like this. You see those trophies hanging up there above the choir stalls, all those flags and things? Those are the bed-sheets, the embroidered fine linen bedsheets bordered with priceless lace made by blind nuns under water in Belgium on which Antonia seduced all those noble ladies in her youth.'

'Under water? We used to have underwater sex in California.'

'And in Acapulco, too, lots of places. Capri, for instance. Lots.'

'Not with ladies as noble as these. They don't exist any more.'

WOMEN YES
MEN NO NO!
WE'RE THE SISTERS
OF SAPPHO!

'Oh, c'mon Freddy! You got your cowboy boots on, let's do a stomp!'

'I'd just like to draw your attention to Antonia's collection which runs all the way from this iron chastity belt which she cut off the girl with an acetylene torch . . .'

'Was she burnt bad?' asked Poochie eagerly. 'The girl, I mean.'

'Not at all,' snapped Freddy very sharply. 'Antonia is expert at whatever she does.'

'I was a pretty good welder. I welded some girls up.'

'Countess Bathory, we prefer not to even *hear* about your exploits. Antonia never even singed a pair of silk panties in her whole career. There, in those glass-topped museum show-cases, you'll see her collection of scalps.'

YO HO HO
'N' FIE FO FUM!
TEE HEE HEE
WE'RE NOT SO DUMB!

'Scalps?' I shuddered.

'Hair pieces, actually, made up for her by her wigmaker. She always shaved the delta of Venus of her lovers to prepare them for her big number, *le Coup du Colonel*, as we call it in French.'

'I didn't understand about that when you were telling that story about Morocco just now. What was it she did and how does she do it?'

'Well, my dear, it's supposed to be a secret, you under-stand, but Elaine here claims she read an article about it in a back issue of *Playgirl*.'

'No, not an article, a letter. There was a letter enquiring about it and an answer from the Letters Editor who said that she *had* to admit that the technique exists but she could *not* really recommend it *too* highly because, while it does produce simply *titanic* orgasms, it *can* be dangerous, even fatal.'

'Is that why it's supposed to be such a secret?'

'No no no! Antonia is the soul of probity, the very *soul* of it! She *always* tells her lovers beforehand that it can be fatal.'

'Why do they do it, then? Why do they go through with it, submit to it?'

'Well, I can only suppose that it's like that funny fish the Japanese eat and pay a big price for it although everyone knows that just one nibble of it can knock you down dead, if you get the wrong one.'

'But that's the Japanese! That's not us. We wouldn't eat it.'

'Some people wouldn't even eat pussy.'

'Why Ms Waterbee! That's really coming right out with it, isn't it?'

'That's what I always believe in doing but Poochie won't always let me. She likes to do me especially when I'm having my period. It's the blood she likes. What you do is you blow into her vagina instead of just sucking and licking and nibbling on her clitoris. You blow into her Fallopian tubes as hard as you can and as much air as you can. Some have been known to use a bicycle pump but that's downright dangerous. You press in there to close her tubes off and you bring her to clitoral orgasm manually at the same time so she comes and she comes and she comes ... how should I say it, organically. All over! Soul and body! Body and soul. What's dangerous is that you can force a bubble of air into her bloodstream and when it gets up into her brain it blows it, blows your brain just like that. *Pow!* an embolism. You're dead. Sometimes I really wonder if it's worth it but Poochie really digs it, digs the danger of it, she's so adventurous still and at her age, why, she's ageless.'

'Aren't we all,' sniffed the duchess. 'But tell me, Ms Waterby...'

'The name is Water*bree*, duchess.'

'Ah, yes, well now, what I wanted to ask you was: is that how you, ah, came over to us? Doing that?'

'No, Poochie and I were doing a Napoleon on the Ramparts when the ramparts fell in on us.'

'I thought you could do Napoleon on the Ramparts only with a man, hmmm?'

'Why? Why only a man? Anything a man can do my Poochie can do as well or better. She's got a 21-centimetre clitoris.'

'Twenty-one centimetres, wow! How much is that in inches?'

'You work it out for yourself. It's plenty, I can tell you. Lots of girls just can't take it. It goes right up into their uterus and pokes a hole in it. They die of it. She's lost lotsa girls that way in her day.'

'From what I read in the *International Herald Trib* published right here in Paris, France, she stands to lose something else, her American citizenship. You've seen this article I picked up back there in the john of the hotel?'

'The john?'

'Yes, the Turkish toilet on the half landing in the stairs. It's just a scrap I pulled off the nail in the wall. You remember. Here's the headline that caught my eye immediately: COUNTDOWN FOR A COUNTESS, it says:

Department of Immigration officials are preparing to wit!idraw US citizenship from a notoriously anti-Semitic female vampire who was once walled up in her own Transylvanian castle by a family council. It was reported that the gutters outside her townhouse in Vienna ran red with blood when she gave a party. Related to royalty, Countess Erzavetta Bathory was a legendary beauty who was said to bathe in the blood of her victims in order to rejuvenate herself regularly. Walled up in 1754, she was liberated by a premature OSS commando of female operatives who broke into her impregnable old castle in 1945. She was interrogated before the Allied Denazification Commission and freed in the custody of an American GI she married, Flight Sergeant Timidity Titmarsh of Tuscaloosa. She . . .'

'OK, duchess, you can stop right there!' screamed Ms Wetherbree. 'All that's the same old shit they always've been handing out about poor Poochie since forever. May I also point out to you that joining the NSDAP (the National Socialist Department of Applied Psychometry), like they say she did, was not automatically a passport to the Nuremberg trials, but akin to joining a union and for the same reason, to get a job. That's why my Poochie is working to this day, thanks to the Americans. She is the Director of the Missaroula, Mississippi Blood Bank and proud of it. That's her motto, Black Blood *tastes* Better.'

'Oh my dear, this sounds all too familiar,' sighed General Whang, very heavy. She was always very heavy. 'Dear me, what will the duchess say?'

'Whang,' snapped the duchess, 'you're not all that funny. This's all Antonia's fault for inviting just about anybody.'

'But who is Antonia, who is she that all the dykes decry her?'

'Oh tell us!'

'Yes, tell us. Tell us now, we can't wait.'

'Where does her loot come from, anyway?'

'Her loot comes from the Longfinger Legacy but you're not supposed to talk about it lightly in this house, not where Antonia can overhear you.'

'Why not? What's the matter with her money?'

'It's because of where it comes from. Antonia's great-grandfather may have invented the perforations in toilet-paper, but his son became the first senator and practically owned half the state of Montana, the upper part near the Canadian border where he put in the railroad and built the High Level Bridge over the Milk River. He owned the whole North Side of Milk River City and Antonia still does. Never goes there anymore, of course, but she still owns it lock stock and barrel. It's inalienable real estate although her father when he was alive more than once tried to get his hands on it, Mario Malapata, the Duke of Darkness, he was called. That's what you get for marrying penniless princess from Palermo, *mafiosi*, all of them. Mario was no exception, sheer bad news all the way to the cemetery. Antonia's poor mother eventually committed suicide in Capri. Gave a big luncheon party around the swimming pool for her friends and opened her veins. Very painful. Have you ever had a haemorrhage? You'd know what I mean if you had. Your arteries ache all over. Those old Romans were even tougher than you might think they were, let me tell you,' said Freddy.

'So, our Antonia is Italian, is she?'

'No no no! She's American through and through. Her money is American money just like my money and that's what counts, isn't it? That's how she became such a great collector and you know what happens to collectors eventually, don't you? No? Why, what happens to collectors is that they get collected by still bigger collectors. You see, this lofty banqueting hall we are in is actually the chapel of Joan of Arc and all those banners and flags you see up there in the flickering shadows on the gilded beams of the ceiling are sheets, bedsheets. Those tattered silken sheets run up like yachting signals are, are, are pennants made of satin and silk panties bordered with priceless lace made in Belgium by blind nuns under water, the likes of which will be seen no more on earth. Antonia never went in for rough trade until later. Her conquests in her best years were all titled ladies and superstars throughout the centuries. Apart from that moth-eaten suit of red flannel long-johns belonging to the Maid of Orleans herself, the Virgin and Martyr, all those trophies are topnotch trifles from topnotch trade. None of their rough homespun or bleached flour sacks roughly stitched together nor the short and simple flannels of the poor for Antonia. No *siree*! No, Madame, I mean! There hang the slips shifts camisoles camiknickers and corset covers, the bodices bustles breastpads and chestpads, and even a chastity belt or two that she collected, partly eaten away in front by the urine but still quite a barrier that she took a nail-file to and worked and *worked* over. Antonia got one of them off a penniless lord who had locked his wife into it. Antonia scalped her. Her collection of scalps, as I said, is laid out in these handsome glass museum cases running around the room in alphabetical order from Z to A, Zenobia to Antonia, herself. Ah, there she is now!'

'Where where where? We don't see her!'

'My mistake. Sorry. She is supposed to materialize up there on the high altar. All the lovely ladies whose locks lie up there in the showcase have to show up first, though. This is the one party no Gurl can afford to miss in the interests of her own immortality. Tonight, we are all going to be catalogued but forever and ever. We'll all be in Antonia's book.'

'Antonia's book! Whatever book is that? What kind of book and why do we have to be in it?'

'You'll see. She's going to read it to us.'

'Oh goody!'

'Goody? I don't know about *that*,' said Freddy firmly. 'There's one thing I can tell you is this: if life is a party or should be, well, hell is a party where the hostess holds you here by the balls or the short hairs as it were and reads her book to you.'

'Oh migawd!'

'Yes, indeed, well you may say it. Oh migawd, what are we in for?'

'In for? Well, after the reading we're in for a translation.'

'A trans*lation*? Into what, pray? Japanese? I'm not going to sit still for that!'

'I was using the word a mite pedantically, I confess,' laughed the duchess. 'What I meant is that we are going to be whisked off to sunny California with the rest of these antiques.'

'Antique, yourself. Howzat?'

'Yeah, howzat?'

'Ages and ages ago, Antonia promised Little PG's father and his grandfather before him that she would, on certain feminist conditions naturally, give all this to their Museum in Malibu. And we are all going along with it, just like that.'

'Not me, I'm not!' I spoke up boldly. 'I've just come from

there. That's where I had my last fatal interview with the Big Boss, as he liked to call himself, Little PG Six.'

'What happened?'

'Out on the desert by El Mirage Lake, he tried to run me down, so I shot him. Back in the hotel, I've got the police report on all that. I'm going to take it to Greece with me.'

'Greece? Why Greece?'

'To intercept him. I'm on a mission for the feminist Movement I belong to in California. Oh, it's all too long to explain but it's important, mighty important to all of us, believe me, all us girls. How do I get back to the Bardo?'

'That's easy, my dear,' offered Madame Rachou. 'You're *in* the Bardo, still in the Bardo, right now. There is one little technical difficulty, though, since the Museum Movers took out your Room Eight.'

'And how about my things? Where's my report?'

'Your old broken black suitcase stuffed with papers was taken up one flight to Room Fifteen directly above you on the stairs.'

'I never had a black suitcase. What do you mean? Who broke it?'

'They had orders to bundle up all the loose papers they found and put them in Room Fifteen.'

'Loose papers?' I screech. 'They must be all mixed up by now and my pages were not even numbered. I've got a real story to tell, the real lowdown on that little male chauvinist pig, PG Six, and by now my report must have lost all its narrative flow.'

'Oh, dear,' murmured Madame Rachou. 'That's what comes of all these new-fangled shuffle-ups and cut-ins.'

'What do you *mean*?' I scream.

'Oh, people changing sex in midstream and all that. If you go on upstairs to Room Fifteen to retrieve your manuscript, since it's already week three and that's his floor now, you're going to run into him again.'

'Who?'

'PG Six.'

CHAPTER THREE
FLOOR THREE
WEEK THREE
ROOM FIFTEEN

'This isn't a room, it's a cage,' I growl at Madame Rachou when she pops her fuzzy blue head into Room Fifteen. 'With those iron bars on the window, it's a prison cell. It's as cold as the grave and there's almost no light in here. I can't live like this.'

'No, of course not,' she smiles over-sweetly, 'you're dead. But don't blame me, my dear, blame yourself.'

'I seem to have heard that line before,' I admit glumly. 'Someone smart is always telling me that.'

'Yes, I guess,' she sighs. 'But after all it was you who ordered your world-movers to take out the old hotel to fit it into your mighty museum of memory. Since they tore out the three floors below us here, everything has been all askew in the Bardo. I've had to move up here myself and abandon the bistro. There will be no more entries or exits. Everything I could salvage from the past down below is stacked up here around you, all the loose ends of history, all those loose leaves of manuscript abandoned here by all sorts of writers, like the Beats for example.'

'I know. That's why I've just decided to call my Museum of Museums the Beat Museum. Since my head-on collision with the Ma Movement in California, that sounds better to me than MOM.'

'Well, make the most of it. You'll just have to manage in here for a week.'

'A week?' I exclaim. 'There's no bed. Nothing but all these unnumbered pages of typescript pouring out of this old broken black suitcase.'

'You can sleep on top of those things of Fiona's,' says Madame as she starts to ooze out of the room.

'Fiona's?' I yelp. 'Whose Fiona?'

'Yours,' she comes back, 'the Curator of your Glory that was Greece Department.'

'Assistant Curator, and I fired her. If she shows up here, I'll kill her all over again.'

'Silly,' she says, 'you can't kill the dead. Besides she says she has your power of attorney. Power of eternity, I mean. You'll still have to deal with her and here she is now,' cackles Madame Rachou as she slams the door hard enough to crack the full-length mirror on the back of it, and in the mirror there is Fiona, only a reflection of her, deaf, dumb and blind I hope.

As I stare at her, frozen in horror, she turns into the antique cult statue of Ma which we have in the MOM at Malibu in the Villa de Lerium built for my great ancestor, PG One. He, of course, did not belong to Her or I would not be here but I feel Ma has been after me since I can remember. MA MA MA!

Ma is the Mother goddess, Kybele the Castrator with a broken nose on her powerful bull dyke mug. Wearing a mural crown like the towers and walls of an ancient city, she sits there enthroned with her fleshy thighs spread wide and stained black with the bloody sacrifice of their manhood which her male adepts must cut off and toss up on to her lap. RAH RAH RAH! MA MA MA!

When the Ma Movement grew so strong in California that they invaded my museum to celebrate their bloody rites, I made every effort to chase them. I ordered the Basilica of Kybele in the interior patio of the Villa to be walled up. To my astonishment, this alienated the majority of my own staff. All the women and most of the men, too, turned out to be members of Ma. In the end, it was they who chased me. RAH RAH RAH! MA MA MA! YOU CAN BEAT THE MOM BUT YOU CAN'T BEAT MA!

The sound of their chanting and the snaky music to which they drove themselves into a sacred frenzy drove me to take refuge in the last sacred male sanctuary which I had placed out on the Mojave in El Mirage Lake. I brought over the tiny Greek island of Delos and set it down in this dry lake where I had it protected by a moat flooded with blue tinctured male urine to keep off the Ma people. Only uncastrated adolescent boys and men were allowed on the holy island which the ancient Greeks held to be the birthplace of the blond sun god Apollo. This was to be my last refuge in a world driven mad by Ma. I was on my way out there when the accident happened.

Who has not seen members of the Ma Movement snaking down Sunset Boulevard in the late afternoon when Ra is drowning out in the Pacific to the West as the last-minute shoppers go schlepping along to the Bigboy Supermarkets? Who has not shaken their filthy begging paws from off the sleeve of his sharkskin suit? Who has not angrily refused to drop even a thin dime into the clanking collection-boxes of these expert 'dingers', these newly ordained metragyrtes with heads shaven like monks except for their long toplock of hair? This lock is for Ma to yank them to Her bosom, pitiful specimens that they are in their baggy yellow dhotis sagging between their self-shaven loins like transextites wearing soiled babies' nappies above their smelly yellow Day-glo running shoes. Who has not brushed off these pestiferous painted postulants as persistent as horseflies? Who has not slammed a screendoor in their clownish faces plastered with oriental make-up? Who has not grabbed for his own cock and balls as soon as he hears the mad bloodbeat of their hypnotic trance music coming down Rodeo Drive? Far away in your safe-house in Brentwood you can still hear the distant silver tinkle of their finger cymbals and the insane gnat-whine of their flutes which go dancing along in your inner ear long after the music has stopped. What man in his right mind has ever broken his stride to listen for even one nanosecond to the pernicious doctrine they preach as they run down the street after you batting their false eyelashes like vampire bats? Yet who has not seen the sensational crowds they gather on the corner of Hollywood and Vine or in Times Square or Trafalgar Square, the Place Saint-Michel on the Left Bank in the Latin Quarter of Paris or just about anywhere else? How about that?

Haven't you ever felt a twinge of sick curiosity about Ma yourself?

To set my face against Ma has cost me my Museum of Musuems and my life, everything but this narrow room in the old Bardo Hotel, yet as long as my magical island of Delos still glimmers out there on the golden desert haze of memory, I will not fall into the wombtrap of Ma the Castrator nor be born again except as the sun god, Apollo Himself.

When I paw through this shoal of paper on which I float, my eye is caught by a scrap of newsprint. It amuses me to remember or think I remember that I once cut this out of a paper myself:

> You and I are not who we claim to be. We are not who we were only yesterday nor are we who we will be tomorrow. Our bodies are by no means static. No living thing can be at rest. A different person looks back at you each morning from the mirror. We produce a whole new skin surface each week. The entire lining of the mouth is washed down and digested with every meal. Each blink of an eye flushes hundreds of cells down the tearducts. All in all, we lose a soup plate full of cells every day and this loss has to be made good.

I re-read this several times and each time I laugh. Who can be at rest, ever? Who looks back at you from the mirror? Have I eaten the entire lining of my mouth as a sadistic nurse in the Horsepistol, what I called Horror Hospital, told me an AIDS victim had done, eating away his own lips in a night of agony? And how is this loss to be made good at this late date?

The next thing I pick up is a couple of pages torn out of a glossy gay magazine with an amusing line drawing by Keith Haring. The text is about a bullfighter who comes a dark splotch of come on his pale silk panties . . . when he sees the bull with a bloodshot eye lolling his scum-covered tongue at him like a lover in a leather bar. (See illustration.)

He knows that the bull has eyes to really get him by ramming the razor-sharp horn that he happens to favour right up his rectum. *Olé!* He knows he is Deadly Diego the Diestro and the bull knows it too. In response, his own big hard smelly uncircumcised cock throbs through its knot of varicose veins. Both he and the bull stand there panting for the moment of Truth with the Little Death of orgasm for one and the final spasm out there in the sandy arena for the other. The whole arena is holding its breath while these two, man and beast, measure each other. Man vs Beast. Since the Ace of Spades is up, you play it.

What you do is, you slowly pluck your *espada*, your ace up the sleeve, out of the red rag wrapping it. Don't bat an eyelash between you and your bull's eye. Stay on target. Sighting your right eye straight down your blue blade directly into the small depression over his left collarbone, you lean into your sword with the whole weight of your body behind it. Ideally, the bull should lean into it, too, taking it directly into his heart, *recibiendo*. The thrust should take you through the living coral of his lungs into the palpitating cavern of his truly magnificent body as big as a truck, right down into the flaring pump of his scarlet heart. That's all there is to it. What are you waiting for? Your blade should slip into him up to the hilt. Before he can raise his horns to toss you into the bleachers, he drops dead. You have taken his life from him harmoniously, amorously. Loving you and you only at that moment of truth, the colossal crowd surrounding you bursts into cheers.

Your personal pay-off is an orgasm, the Little Death right out there in the arena, the bull's-eye of all eyes. You ejaculate into your skintight pink sexy silk kneepanties and ten thousand throats scream up into hysteria as they see the dark patch spread into the bull's blood smeared across your crotch. Chicuelo Segundo was a great expert at this. Big bumbling bull stumbles and crumbles to his baggy knees, drunk on his own blood, coughing up a king's ransom in rubies. As he blows out his last great bubble of blood it bursts and spreads out like a ragged red flag on the sand where it blackens instantly as he falls at your feet. For a solemn second or two, you gaze down on death with bowed head. Then you lift your chin proudly raising both arms slowly in a magnificent theatrical gesture you practised for hours in front of your full-length mirror back in your local hotel. You take off your hat to your public, turning gracefully in a full circle on your slippered heel, inviting more and more applause from the public piled up on the tiers of the ring surrounding you. Cheering you to the skies, they break out a pentecostal host of white handkerchiefs like clouds of doves taking off when the canon is fired at noon in front of the fucking old Seville cathedral. Today is your day. You are its hero. Your triumphal tour around the ring is carpeted with carnations. Strong silent Spanish men smile a tight smile as they sail their expensive Cordoban flat hats at you like frisbees. Their women go mad as maenads at full moon time.

That is one way it can go. The other way is awful. When your bad day comes, you lunge in to lean on your sword and it hits bone. The steel buckles under you. A bullfighter's *espada* has been known to bend like a bow as it skids over bone and flips into the air like a spring. In Cordoba once, this *torero*'s sword flew through the air like a glittering arrow while everyone was gawking up at it. His *novia*, his promised one, was there in the best box with her long greasy black hair over her arms and her arms full of flowers, his heavily embroidered cape draped over the rim of the ring in front of her. Was the sun in her eyes as she gawked up open-mouthed like the rest of them? The slim blade came whistling down out of the dazzling sky and straight down her throat, passing right through her. Her lover's *espada* pinned her to the wooden seat she was sitting on, right through her asshole.

Trouble is, at that moment the crowd's red-hot rivet of attention is fixed on her and no one is paying any attention to you. No one but the bull, that is. The bull has just impaled you, too, right up the rectum with the horn that he favours, and tossed you as high as a basketball scoreboard. What goes up must come down and you land on his other horn after turning a full somersault in the bright air. Now he can swing you around a couple of times before flinging you with all the force of his bullneck against the wooden *barrera* or he can twirl you

94

around a couple of times like a friendly fistfucker might do to you one Saturday night in The Mineshaft or The Tubs on Christopher Street in New York. You can thank your lucky stars that the bull's horns have been 'shaved', as they call it, filed down. The surgeons who are waiting for you in the wings will have less trouble with nasty old infectious splinters of bone when they get you laid out on the operating table.

> *Then the Lord of Death will place round thy neck a rope and drag thee along. He will cut off thy head, tear out thy heart, pull out thine intestines* ... (Oh! Ouch! That hurts!) ... *lick up thy brain, drink thy blood, eat thy bones, etc. but thou wilt be incapable of dying. Even when thy body is hacked to pieces, it will revive again* ... (Oh no! Not again! C'mon, lemme outta here!) ... *and again and again.* (Oh! Oh! Oh!) *The repeated hacking will cause intense pain and unbearable torture.* (Oh! Noooo!)
>
> *Bardo Thodol,* The Tibetan Book of the Dead

Next thing you know, you wake up screaming. You are alone in a bone-bare room under a glaring white light, *The* Clear White Light! Leather and chains buckle you down on an icy cold chromium bedstead. You know where you are, of course. You might as well go along with it. You are in the Ultimate Cancer Ward at the far end of the Yellow Wing. Your veins have been pulled out of your arms like garden worms and attached to gravity drips of fresh blood hanging from stainless steel gallows on each side of the bed. Your arteries ache. You know what you are here for. Yes, you do. Your big mouth, that's what's done it. You have been talking too much, from away back, blabbing your secrets and theirs away to your other self, that feminine one. Naturally, She blabbed. She told them all, so now your contract is going to be terminated with extreme prejudice. And why not? The Agency is taking care of people like you, everywhere. They have just snatched your old asshole out from under you and now they want the rest. It is their due. Sucker, pay up!

Violet, that blue-assed baboon dressed up as a nurse, made you sign for the operation, remember? Then she shot you up with BZ, their new drug they call soul-destroying, as if you had one. The two great antique Greek surgeons in pale green chitons and masked, Professor Kokalos (Dr Bones) and Professor Haemos (Dr Blood), ripped out your rectum with the aid of an electric apple-corer and sawed off the end of your coccyx, that little knuckled tailbone at the end of your spine, in order to get in there and scoop you out like a rotten old canteloupe. With one rubber-gloved fist up your ex-asshole and the other plunging down through a nine-inch incision from your sternum to your shaved pubis, they gleefully shook hands with each other in the depths of your belly ... (Dr Livingstone, I presume) ... darker than darkest Africa. *Les petites mains de la haute couture, les biaiseuses de chez Paquin* were called in to stitch you up again, all but your stoma which will never heal because it is round, round as a Maria Theresa silver thaler. This is your anus-praeter, your brand new artificial anus. Get to love it as fast as you can. There it is down there on the left side of your gut, gurgling away like an obscene baby mouth drooling a long snake of blood, mucus and shit into a transparent plastic bag attached to the skin of your stomach by a sticky ring of karaya gum. Look on it rather as a shiny wet red tea-rose of tender intestinal tissue with its puckered border of stitches oozing tears of blood like dewdrop rubies around the edge of its petals. In order to achieve this expensive artistic effect, they have moved your original mothering navel, the bellybutton you were born with that last time, they have moved it over four inches to the right, your tight right hand. At the middle point of the suture, they inserted deep into your central chankra a new umbilical cord of plastic tubing to drain off your new navel.

You have been reborn. You will find your new name on the board in the matron's office, when you can get there and read it. If you can read.

Paramedical Report. Sir William Van Burroon, Kt (Knight),

FRCS (Fellow of the Royal College of Surgeons), OBE (Order of the British Empire), the Queen's own proctologist (a proctologist deals only in assholes), is to be assisted in this operation by his colleague Professor Benjamin Benway, OM (Order of Merit) and the usual competent staff of doctors and nurses. When what is left of you is wheeled in on a trolley into the operating theatre, the floodlights go up. The cast is assembled and waiting for you. You are still the star of the show and what they are going to do to you is going to be drastic, a drama. Forget about the glamour of the bullring, that farce of the Fiesta Brava. This is the real thing and you are now cast in the role of the bull on his way to the butcher's. Nurses in funny starched caps are playing the roles of *monosabios* who clean up the arena after each bloody encounter. Four young cape-swinging interns are your *cuadro*. The two pre-eminent proctologists are your *picadores*, mounted on the rickety old warhorses of their bloodstained profession. Burroon and Benway are standing there masked, robed in pale green operating smocks (chosen because blood blackens on them immediately). In a trice, their sinewy young assistants have you trussed up and hung by your heels from two steel hooks attached to pulleys in the ceiling, to hoist you up with your thighs spread apart, like the carcass in an abattoir.

Under the hot overhead lights, sweat is already pouring down into the two surgeons' eyes above their masks. Will they be able to see what they are doing, properly? They are about to perform on you an abdominal colostomy and complete perineal resection with full amputation of the anus and rectum right up to where the bull's horn tore up your sigmoid colon and further. The anaesthetist is Sir William's blue baboon assistant, Violet, the only woman he ever loved. She is tenderly wiping the sweat from his eyes. Violet is wearing a gas mask from World War I to protect her from the poison gases she is about to administer to you. Because there was no time to give you your premedication, Violet has tossed down your lytic cocktail herself: *10 mg Doperidol, 100 mg Pethidine, 50 mg Phenergan, and 0.4 mg Scopolamine*. As a result, she is feeling delightfully woozy. She prepares an induction of *400 mg Scopalomine* for you and fuzzily fusses around unable to make up her mind what in the hell to use for your intubation. She ponders on: *100 mg Suxamethonium* by spray, or perhaps better by injection. Or should she stick to a spray of *8 mg Pancuronium*? She can't decide. She might as well use both of them. And how about a little *Halothene* while she is at it . . . why not? Personally, she digs all of them. She has her tank of nitrous oxide by her side and her *Trichloroethylene* as well as her *Halothene* for maintenance with a milligram or two more *Pancuronium* in reserve, just in case. She takes a deep sniff of her gas tank and practically floats up to the ceiling.

'Steady on, old girl,' Sir William mutters from behind his mask. He and Benway are standing by, looking like jade idols with pink rubber-gloved hands held out stiffly in front of them to avoid contagion as much as possible. However, it is well known in the trade, around the hospital, and in local medical circles, that Professor Van Burroon does not truly believe in what he calls 'the germ theory', scoffing it off as nineteenth-century pseudoscientific nonsense. Mr Benway is sneezing behind his surgical mask because Violet cut his cocaine with Saniflush . . . to be sure he will keep his eye on the old ball. Benway's business in hand is to slice open your abdomen from stem to sternum while Van Burroon eradicates your rear end. Somethin' awful. You go under the anaesthesia to the *bleep bleep bleep* of the electronic monitors burping like Star Wars in a pinball parlour. Over the insistent sexy sigh of the respirator, you can just catch a snatch of the antiphonal chorus of surgical shamans going into the litany of their favourite operation, a perineal resection with full amputation of . . .

'. . . retractors . . . surgical scissors . . . suction . . . sponge . . .'

An hysterical voice breaks in over the intercom: *Prepare for admittance of a case of bubonic plague . . . over . . .*

'. . . retractors . . . scissors . . . suction . . . silver soup spoon . . .'

Another voice screams: *Stand by for an emergency ... terrorists are attacking the Horse-pistol ... over ...*

'No!' snaps Sir William to Violet, 'leave that lay, that's the apple-corer.'

'... suction ... silver spoon ... apple-corer...'

Man the mains! There has been a glooop!

'... retractors ... haemostat ... clamps...'

There is about to be a power failure ... break out your flashlights!

'... needle ... catgut ... spiderweb poultice...'

'Violet, my dear, do give me just one sniff of your nitrous oxide. I'm feeling wobbly.'

The arc lights flicker and fail ... then come on again.

'... radical excision ... perineal resection ... full amputation of the rectum and sigmoid colon up to...'

There has been an outbreak of encephalitis in Jex Blake Ward ... over.

Emergency! Emergency! There has been an explosion in ... over.

'Violet, my dear, do give me just one more sniff of your nitrous oxide. I'm *still* feeling wobbly.'

'Dr Benway, I presume,' mutters Sir William, grimly. Like your friendly fistfucker, he has his right hand and forearm up your asshole as far as his elbow. Good ole Doc Benway, on the other hand, has entered your abdomen through the incision he made in your belly from your umbilicus to your shaven pubis. How happy they are to meet up inside you! Like the two famous explorers at the Zambesi Falls on the confines of the Congo, they shake hands warmly, deep within your abdominal cavity, darker than darkest Africa. Congratulating each other on this fortuitous encounter, they exchange spare parts of your colon. You are not supposed to assist at this historic meeting but, oddly enough, you do. You are there. So much the worse for you.

The anaesthetic poisons Violet is administering to you are the countdown to death. Your lungs are beginning to rattle: Cheney-Stokes breathing they call it, the death rattle. Alarmed, she shoots you a little oxygen to revive you and it revives you only too much. Suddenly ... zippo! The bull has just tossed you up again like a basketball. From up there near the ceiling in the shadows above the hooded arc lights, you are looking down on your own bloody carcass stretched out ... laid out on the operating table like a half-dissected corpse. You panic. Frantic with fear, you wonder how in the hell you are ever going to get back in there again, with all those tubes they have thrust down your throat, up your nostrils and into your veins, let alone all those stainless steel instruments Van Burroon is wielding with his left hand while he reels around with his fist and forearm up your giggy like a wire brush.

There is only one thing to do: scare the shit out of him. Make him pull out of there pronto! So, you nosedive down to jump into his eyes, half-blinded by sweat and, just then, he withdraws his bloody arm and hand from the shitty raw hamburger of his and *your* rumpsteak, to let Violet wipe off his brow and give him another snootful of her nitrous oxide. 'OOOOOP!' she cries as she glances back around to see you passing out of your body. So she clamps her respirator back over your face and starts pressing your arteries to bring you around. There you are again. You made it. But why in the hell did you want to? How very dumb of you, not to turn in a badly wrecked bodyjob like that, when you had the chance to. Don't you know a lousy deal when you see one? Whatever possessed you?

When Violet came back with her hypodermic needles tinkling on top of her trolley of drugs, he asked her what his new name was but she simply shook her perky little starched cap at him as she flipped back his bedclothes to take an impertinent peek into his stoma. Before he could scream, she had ripped the plastic shitbag off his belly to plunge her long hairy middle finger into the hole in his gut. Then she rolled the boy over to take a look up his ex-asshole, loosening one of the buckles on his restraint to do so. This gave him the leverage he needed to loosen his good arm and grab a hypo from the tray on the top of her trolley, ramming the hooked needle hard into her hairy behind, shooting her up with her own BZ, apparently. She dropped to the floor with a little whimpering sigh and was still. He undid his bondage belts, sat up slowly and dropped his wasted legs over the side of the bed.

His feet dangle down there like sand bags at the ends of these rubbery legs of his. Will they hold him? He falls back across the bed, limp with exhaustion, but his hand hits the drug trolley, causing a shower of pills to cascade down on him. All he has to do is open his mouth and swallow them. Within a matter of seconds, he is a new man. Is that his new name, Newman? Norman Newman? No, that would be some-body else, now wouldn't it? From New Jersey, perhaps. Not New Jersey. He knows he is a Californian. Wait now, it's coming to him. But he can't wait. He must get the hell out of here as fast as he can out of this bad movie: *Horror Hospital*, directed by Antony Balch.

He pulls the drips out of his veins and stands up very gingerly, naked as a newborn babe. Tottering around to the other side of the bed where Violet lies unconscious on the floor, he painfully pushes his swollen feet into her high-heeled white plastic pumps. Her blond wig fits him perfectly but he cannot get decently into her starched white smock, so he drapes himself in a sheet and sallies forth into the hall corri-dor. Panic has broken loose out there. An emergency! Bells are ringing, buzzers buzzing, lights flashing off and on as mad-dened crowds of orderlies, nurses, doctors and patients, drug pushers, peddlers of obscenity and a basketball team of naked Pima Indians (see illustration) swarm all over each other. Grabbing a ride on a passing motorized trolley, he gathers speed as the crowd divides in terror in front of him, sweeping down the white halls of the hospital and through big glass double doors which fly open as he is pitched out into a garden, a vast semi-tropical garden which he recognizes immediately. There on the outskirts of Palmdale, laid out to serve as the proper setting for the Temple of Jupiter, are the Zappeion gar-dens from Athens, Greece not Athens, Ohio.

Happy memories! It had always been his favourite cruising ground when he was not in training for the basketball team.

But what if he ran into someone he knew! What would they think if they saw him in this tatty drag outfit, limping down the shady alleys under the oleanders? He had always been strictly trade, played it cool. Now they might take him for some kind of Mary. The chilling thought suddenly strikes him: maybe he is a girl, this time around. That reminds him of something: hasn't he been a girl, a great big basketball-playing girl, somewhere or other and recently? He runs into the bushes, literally jumping out of those horrible high-heeled shoes, and pulls up his draped sheet to see what he's got. To his great relief, he sees a cock and balls hanging there and it's not a bad deal, about the same size as the last one. To his surprise, though, this time he is not circumcised. He must have escaped at least that trauma, somewhere along the road. But a much bigger surprise is down there in store for him. His belly is smoothly muscled and flat, no sign of the stoma. He is whole again. He produces a sharp abdominal isolation and gives a big sigh. The muscles stand out like marble.

But he really must get into some other threads, he is thinking as he fingers the sheet he is wrapped in. At one end, it has a band of purple running through it and a gold fringe bordering it. He fingers the imperial material and sees it is silk. This is no ordinary sheet, he laughs to himself, and why? Because it fits him. It fits him when he throws it in a certain way around his waist and then over his left shoulder, just so, and it is a garment. So, now he knows who he is, more or less, even if he can't remember his name yet. He must have been brought over to southern California by the Glory that was Greece and the Grandeur that was Rome Department.

He remembers with a hoarse laugh what happened to Clarence Cobb, the queer curator of GG and GR who was always cruising up and down these dark alleys like leafy tunnels beneath semi-tropical trees. The poor man was found crucified one morning in the barbed wire, down by the temple of Jupiter Thunderer. The remaining handful of tall Corinthian columns, all that was left of the ancient Athenian cathedral first restored so long ago by the Emperor Hadrian, had been set out on the edge of the Mojave Desert beyond the city limits of Palmdale. Beyond, glimmering through the Californian haze, he could see the newly cleaned Parthenon glittering like an ad for toothpaste on top of the red butte (see note, p. 104) at Little Rock. (Zip code: C A. 93434.)

The temple of Jupiter stands just off California state highway 18, before you get to the gate of Air Force Plant 2. Consequently, it has long been a hangout for rival bike-boy battalions, the Hets and the Peds. The Hets being straights aligned with Hell's Angels, the Peds being gay S and M. That poor old curator – what was his name? – simply walked into it. Anyone in southern California should know better than to go skulking down around the temple of Jupiter on his Harley, at night and on foot. The headless naked messengers of the old gods (see illustration) are tearing through the night on their Triumphs, their BMWs, magic hotrods and Yamahas. The Hard Hadrian Hotrodders are looking for a beautiful teenager to sacrifice him, or better, persuade him to sacrifice himself to a crocodile they have holed up in a Palmdale swimming pool. The curator – wasn't his name Clarence Something or other or was that the one in the French Drawings Department? Well, anyway, some of the Peds had run into him at a demonstration and, on mention of their meeting place, the temple of Jupiter–Jove, he had told them the story of the emperor Hard Hadrian and his lovely Lydian lover, Antinous. Shortly after giving the order for the temple to be restored, they had left together for a winter in Egypt, cruising slowly up and down the Nile on the imperial barge. Everyone remembers what happened. The poor kid, getting on a bit, long in the tooth at twenty, it is true, felt it his duty to sacrifice himself to the crocodile god of the river so that Hadrian could go on plundering the breadbasket of Egypt. Until that all happened, it had been a lovely cruise. The barge was so big that its decks were laid out like hanging gardens planted with alleys of fruit trees leading to fountains of wine.

All the flowers in the gardens were white, to glimmer in the moonlight, and only heavily scented ones were planted: tuberoses, datura, nicotiana, gypsophila, phlox. Beds of gardenias were laid out on the deck to lie on. Bowl-sized magnolia blossoms were presented to guests with pearls rolling around in their calyxes like dewdrops. All the perfumes of Arabia flowed over the cataracts of the Nile and swept about the prow or the stern of Hadrian's barge, fore-and-aft. Smoky incense culled from the amber drops of 1,000-year-old coniferous trees in the Hadramaut, hung in the flowering orange trees, caught up in nets of jasmine vine. One simply swooned under the moon or was it just some old battered lantern hung aloft to light poor travellers to their distress? Beneath all these heavy odours lay the greatest smell of them all, man-sweat. Our barge swam slowly upstream under the power of 5,000 magnificently muscled body builders chained to our oars below the decks and this odour, this manly musk, came up to us in delirious waves to the soft beat of the great drum which commanded their stroke with the very rhythm of the sexual act. Everyone on board was in a red-hot state of rut.

He looks down and sees that his silk sheet with the purple thread is hanging over his erection. He drops into the Nile to be eaten by the crocodile and become immortal.

NOTE: *The red butte of Little Rock*: Pronounced *'Littler Rock'* by the staff of Free Greek security guards who came over with the Parthenon. The Parthenon was a great bargain which the Museum acquired by cable from the last Greek government before its ultimate collapse. The Parthenon was in very bad shape. Not only was it eroded by pollution and tourism but the Greeks had been informed by the Turkish government that they planned to *'emulate the Venetian admiral Morosini who made your Parthenon what it is today by bombarding it in 1678'*.

On hearing this, Little PG Six rang his world movers, *Interdead Interrational* as we all called them. They moved everything for him: Abu Simbel to

Brentwood to serve as the PG Family Mausoleum, the Great Wall of China to run along the line of the Los Angeles aqueduct past China Lake and the Diamond Mountains all the way to Death Valley, the Italian Renaissance to Ravenna, CA., the British Museum to Acton, CA., the Agora of Athens to Palmdale to serve as a shopping mall, etc. etc. Our I. I. Movers had a new man in Greece called Lambros Karnavalos, phone Athens: 30.1.941-80.66, who ran an ad featuring himself in gym shorts carrying the Parthenon on his shoulders (see illustration). It read: *'And for my next amazing feat . . . I propose to do this at a rate that won't leave you in ruins.'*

Logistics apart, the outbreak of Armageddon made things infinitely more complicated but all that much more urgent. Whole and entire foreign museums had to be moved along with their curators, conservators and security guards. (See note on *Guides*.) Some of these guides, such as the Egyptian ones notably, had thousands of years of experience with pilgrims and tourists behind them: behind the tourists. They had to be brought over without their wives. Coming from some of the most sensual countries in the world, what began as a hardship for them became a boon to the California gay world, especially the passive Peds.

Under what we call The New Dispensation, anything and everything can be moved better at night. When everyone is sleeping, when no one is looking, when their guards are down and they have been thoroughly defeated, anything is possible any time. The Original Donor was himself an original, unique of his kind. So bold was he that he stole the Louvre and sent it to Arkansas, before moving it out to San Fernando Valley where it belongs.

NOTE: *Guides*: Whatever your trip may be, guides fuck up your trip. Greek guides from the Parthenon and from the sacred island of Delos where Apollo was born, Turkish guides from the Blue Mosque and the

Topkapi, Syrian guides from the admirable museum in Damascus or the great Roman temple turned into a church turned into a mosque and the guide turned into a lubricious lunatic attacking you sexually in the tomb of Saint John the Golden-mouthed, Iranian guides chasing you through the meagre ruins of Persepolis (now re-erected in toto, high on Ord Mountain at an altitude of 6309 feet) (see note), Egyptian guides who came to California with the treasures of Cairo showing you their splendidly circumcised members behind the mummy cases, rough up-country guides from Luxor chasing you through the forests of phallic columns, lewd and crude Lybian guides from the astonishing ruins of Leptis Magna under a full moon with the Mediterranean lapping at the quay stones of the ancient port in which you both swim with your naked bodies bright from phosphorescence in the warm water, languid Tunisian guides in the Bardo museum at Carthage, with a sprig of jasmine behind one ear under their fuzzy red fezzes, toughen up enough to touch your behind as you bend over to view a set of fifty bronze candelabra made in the form of obscene dinner-table sconces held up by groups of three youths with fully formed female breasts and tiny cocks, Chinese guides . . .

Lulliloo! Lullilooo! Lullilooooo! goes ringing out into the night as squadrons of ululating banshees on power-headed bikes tear through the Zappeion gardens on their 1000cc broomsticks. *Lulliloo! Lulliloo!* Maenads mad on moonshine and mushrooms high up on the San Gabriel Mountains by the Mount Wilson (elevation 5710 feet) Observatory, come roaring down 39a on N2 through Vincent outside of Palmdale. There they took the tar-topped road on the right towards the airport and the Zappeion gardens. The Greek guides, having heard the hunting cry of the Bacchantes long before they ever heard of California, fled in a body, chilled to the bone. A man's blood curdles in his veins and his balls retract right up into his lower abdomen from whence they came down at his adolescence. His penis pulls back, leaving only a wrinkled olive and even that is fair game for the female adepts of Ma the Mother who are riding tonight in full cry, racing up and down and around all southern California under the full moon. He freezes behind the trunk of an ancient oak as the screeching horde sweeps by with such a roar from their bikes that the trees bow down after them and go on shaking their leaves in a tremble for hours.

Next morning, the rollcall of guides revealed that all the Syrians from the Museum of Damascus were missing. The Beverly Hills head office of the Ma Movement announced that they had all joined the cult of Kybele (see note).

NOTE: *Ma-Kybele Cult Movement*: Originating in Syria and Lebanon, this cult caught on in California and now is said to have several million members. The adolescent male and female postulants for membership dance through big city streets to the clashing of cymbals and the tinkling of finger rings with bells bound around their ankles, making their music as the group advances dancing and singing into the supermarkets. Like the Hairy Christmas sect brought back from India by the Beat poet, Gaylord Gainsborough, they have become immensely rich and politically powerful. More than any of the other comparable cults, the Ma Movement has based itself on the extreme feminist fringe, accepting only castrated priests into full membership with women. Priests are self-ordained when they emasculate themselves in front of the goddess whose statue is in the Basilica of Cybele in the right wing of the inner courtyard at the MOM headquarters in Malibu.

We had a hell of a lot of trouble trying to keep those damned Ma people out of the Museum. (See floor plan of the Villa de Lerium.) The cult image and altar of the mother goddess from Baalbek attracted them. They were always trying to sneak in but we made it hard for them. If I may quote from our brochure for a minute, under the heading PARKING RESERVATIONS:

> Advance reservation is recommended for guaranteed admission because visitors who have not made one can enter ONLY if parking is available. Pedestrians are not admitted, except for those arriving by taxi, bicycle or public bus (RTD line 175); bus passengers must present a Museum pass, available from the driver. A reservation, which guarantees one parking space, may be requested by telephoning or writing to the Reservations Office.

Well, we had to tighten up on all that. It was simple. We declared that there was no more parking space because of flooding. It was not entirely untrue. In what had been the old parking space, we were installing the Roman bath from Bath, England and running our newly discovered underground hot spring through it. There was some flooding. A tragedy, eventually.

The Ma people gave themselves away to the guards at the gate. Their saffron yellow garments, their shaven heads with only one long lock left and their grotesquely painted noses gave them away at once. They tried everything, including gliders and an all-out attack by helicopter. They made it.

What they wanted was to dance in front of this statue we have of a big, heavyset, seated woman with a broken nose and a mural crown on her head like the walls and towers of a Roman town (see illustration). 'And all round the walls hung the tools and the balls of the fools who danced in her honour.' I just made that up but you remember the reference. That's what they did for her. They came sashaying and swirling up to her in their sacred trance-dance, singing and stomping the bells on their ankles and clashing their cymbals, gnashing their teeth and rolling their eyes around back into their empty heads, like madmen. I saw them. It was scary. Becoming entranced, they tore off their underpants and went leaping about in nothing but their smelly gym-shoes. God, it was awful! Short-haired priestesses of Ma with plastic bags full of them, went around handing out razor-sharp clam shells. 'Do it! Do it!' they cried. 'Ma Ma Ma!' And they did: they began to do it, really do it. Yes, they cut off their balls and their cocks and threw them on to the lap of the statue we have of the old lady Herself, with her grim broken-nosed prizefighter bulldyke mug up there glaring at them. We all just stood around there, open-mouthed, all of us Museum people, guards and all, paralysed, and let them go to it.

Very unfortunately for them, the Palmdale High basketball team happened to be visiting the Museum in Malibu, as it was laid out then. They were on their way to lay a wreath at the foot of our Praxiteles Apollo where, a short time before, their six-foot-eleven forward named Jimi Dion had been found dead of an overdose. Very unfortunately, as I say for them, they peered into the Syrian Section to see what the hell was going on there and succumbed to the maniacal music. They dropped their drawers and lifted their voices in the hideous hymn to Her. Hostesses from the Ma Movement were right there with the clam shells to help them. As if that were not enough, a group of matrons from the Monterey Garden Club just happened along there with their garden shears. They had been pruning our box hedges and they ran around like mad-women helping out the poor boys who were clumsy or too shy to go through with it. One of these old biddies managed to slice off one of her own nipples in the foray. Scrambling around in the blood on our marble floors, these mad maenads scrambled for the boys' balls, slipping through their fingers like oysters. The Gurls fought tooth and nail for these trophies and not only to toss them onto the lap of the goddess. Many of these were artists, 'artistes' in their own right, and there is money in 'bolos'. They are sold in only the best West Coast galleries.

You know my couplet of 'Fake Blake', don't you?

> *When idle housewives take up Art*
> *The world will really fall apart.*

That just about ties it up. It was another matter tying up those poor kids, I'm telling you. It was hard to get at them in the mêlée between the genuine lady members of the cult and these ambitious lady artists. There is a big market for 'bolos'. (See illustrated catalogue: The Gurls' Gallery Inc. of H'wood Heights.) Mere boys' balls are a drug on the market, but wait until a lady name-artist hangs up a pair snatched from some even fairly well-known misogynist and you see the price shoot up the way the poor man's prick never will again in his lifetime. And there was all this mad music going on. I nearly lost my head, myself. If it hadn't been for Stephen, my old lover in French Painting who pulled me back in time, I might have lost more than that. What is more, it was all happening on prime time live television, and you know how hard it is to resist getting in on that, if you're a mad thing like me, you know. Irresistible ... almost. Only almost, thank God! I'd sooner be crucified than castrated.

The next thing we knew, the Gurls' Gourmet Go-go Group had crashed the party. They sing a lipsmacking song: 'Oysters in September, Caviar in June.' It makes no sense to me but I begin to realize that they are in battle with a sort of subgroup of these sophisticated ladies who prefer testicles roasted on skewers like shish kebab who begin to put down their sisters, screaming, 'Pigs! Pigspisgspigs! That's all you are: Pigs! And you dare to call yourselves gourmets – you're pigs!' At that point, the seven top representatives of the Seven Sisters Syndicate moved in to take over the action. The SSS puts out Balzo and they are as big as Postum, let's say, plenty big although you may not drink Balzo yourself or even know anyone who does. Perhaps your wife slops some down after you have gone to work, as she slumps there in the breakfast nook in her flowered wrapper stained with old make-up, her hair still up in curlers. The Gurls all ingurgitate this foul brew every morning as they slouch around their pads with sixteen butts burning in the ashtrays and the kitchen piled high to the ventilator with dirty dishes among which the colonies of cockroaches play their morning symphony. *Balzo makes you Ballzy*, isn't that the jingle? The Gurls all sit there slumped over the telephone as they 'communicate' for hours with the 'Sisters', like: Ms Mate Killit and Ms Gloria Grindem.

By an incredible piece of luck, Professor Burroon and Doc Benway happened to be passing by the Syrian Section on their way to a poetry reading by their old pal, the Good Gay Poet, Gaylord Gainsborough. Into the breach flew Drs B and B, valiantly assisted by Violet, Benway's blue-assed baboon assistant and lover. These gallant medicos, without even a homoeopathic spiderweb poultice to hand, performed medical marvels, nay, miracles! With the native cunning of cowboys spinning their lariats, they threw ligatures around what these poor lads had left of their sex lives, tying them up with their shoelaces, their ties and belts, even their expensive Sulka silk shirts torn into strips in an attempt to save and sew up a few cocks and balls picked up off the floor. But whose and with what? They had nothing to sew with until a few gay L A dressmakers took out their miniature sewing kits, out from under the wide thirties lapels of their Saint Laurent suits, and then it was: stitch stitch stitch!

And that is what I am afraid of as I run through this darkling wood. The Gurls have apparently swept on past me, probably running on past Pearblossom on Route 18 to cut right on Highway 395 down to Hesperia just for the sheer hell of it and back up through Apple Valley, bypassing Victorville where they are really down on the Gurls, cutting back on old blacktop 395 at Adelanto, then north over the Kramer Mountains, mere hills, to circle around El Mirage as near as they dare. My magic isle of Apollo is inviolable by women because the computer key to the holy holograph can be worked only by the insertion of a penis in erection.

The west wind is raising whitecaps on the unnaturally blue

water of the moat. All I have to do is strip and throw myself headlong into the watery veils of the illusion, perhaps to be drowned and dumped for dead in the detergent foam breaking on the sacred shore. All islands are further away than you think. To land on Delos and be reborn there as the blond sun god is not impossible but you do have to die first. After that, everything is easy.

Waves are produced by a wavemachine of the type you find in the bigger Hollywood pools. The blue is produced by Mictasol. (See note.) In the MOM catalogue it is called IKB or International Klein Blue in honour of the French colourfield artist, Yves Klein, who 'flew through the air like a comet and crashed when a bundle of his accented brushwork blew up in the sky'. See photomontage of the maestro flying out of a second-storey window in Paris.

The colour match is far from perfect and this has brought about endless litigation with the artist's estate. His monochrome paintings, large canvases covered with a single hue of intense deep blue which saturates the eye, his own version of cobalt, aroused both derision and admiration during his lifetime, but the blue was recognizably his own. When first shown, his Greek dealer gave 2,000 super-chic Parisians a blue cocktail. It was a powerful gin and vodka punch laced with Mictasol. Anyone who drank it pissed blue for the next twenty-four hours they spent running to their doctors to find out what had happened to them. And they never forgot it.

NOTE: Mictasol Bleu is a French pharmaceutical product prescribed for prostate troubles, urethritis, uteroovarian congestion, cystitis, pyelonidal cysts, haemorrhoids. It is an excellent genital sedative and urinary antiseptic. It is passed in the urine which it turns blue-green to purple-blue. Each pill contains: 0.02 g of methalene blue and 0.25 g of pulverized seeds of *Malva purpurea*.

All males attached to my MOM were obliged to take Mictasol every day and their urinals drained into the El Mirage moat.

DELOS, Greece, January 19 (UPI)
US archaeologists excavating on the once-sacred island of Delos have unearthed a long vaulted tunnel, perhaps used as a locker-room by visiting athletes and pilgrims who came to bathe in the shallow lake said to be the birthplace of Apollo, the sun god patron of the arts in antiquity.

The walls of the 120 foot tunnel now being cleared by archaeologists of UCLA attached to the PG Museum of Museums are scored with graffiti.

'There are some thirty examples of graffiti in the area of the tunnel excavated so far,' said Professor S. Daedelus, Jr, who directs the dig. 'Names, vows and even sexual boasts were cut into the soft limestone in large angular block letters. It could have been used as a changing or disrobing room. We may be able to give a firm date to the find owing to one name inscribed in bold letters: ION, followed by some twenty-nine other boys' names with a valediction. We know from inscriptions found at Olympia that an Ion was the captain of the basketball team that won at the Olympics around 340 BC and were lost with their coach and their pilot on the flight home by Icarus Airways.'

International Herald Tribune

Ion steps out of the burning plane on to the island of Delos to meet the stern gaze of Spiro Daedalus, the Greek designer of the plane.

'We are turning you over to Immigration,' he snarls. 'You're a Nordic. Tall, blond with blue eyes, you are obviously not a Greek. I hold you responsible for the death of my son Icarus who was flying my plane.'

'The wings were made of feathers stuck together with wax. They fell off when the plane flew too near the sun.'

'You're an illegal immigrant. What's your name?'

'Apollo,' the boy lied glibly, 'and I was born here. When I

was still a child, pirates kidnapped me and sold me to the land where the sun sets in the Western sea. I went to school there and became a basketball player. At the last Olympics, we won.'

'You couldn't be born here. No women are allowed on Delos, ever.'

'My mother was the last one.'

'Break this young man white as marble on the wheel,' ordered D, 'and throw the pieces down there by that pond.'

After that, he heard nothing but the wind and the rain forever and in the distance the snarled and yelping seas as they cast themselves in grief and anger on the bold anfractuous shores of Delos. Soughing in summer, the soft breezes mourned for him and the blue seas whipped themselves into a froth when the Meltemi, the west wind, mourned him in frenzy while the white horses of his uncle Poseidon raced along the bare beaches of Delos through the tattered surf.

This tall tale was told and retold. The legend of Apollo grew as legends will. He was not dead and would never die. Everyone in the ancient world believed he had been born on the island of Delos. He became a star, an immortally young god on earth, the ever-young god of male beauty. All the young surfers on the seas of the world wanted to look like him, have a body like his, wear their hair the way he did, that classical cut with duckass and sideburns. They wanted to go nude or dress like him in faded levis the colour of his eyes, wearing leather jackets and filthy scuffed running shoes. In California, Greek gods grow well. Naked Greek gods in leather and chains can come roaring up your drive after midnight on their Harleys glistening with chrome, sitting astride their folded levis as they roar through the night. (See illustration.) With penises rampant, they can throw themselves into your pool to cool themselves off on a hot afternoon in Hollywood Hills. Or, if you are lucky, they can crash right through your screendoor while you are taking a snooze, to arouse you. Naked Greek gods in the kitchen raiding the icebox (see illustration), Greek gods singing in the shower. You can photograph them as they lounge on your couch playing with themselves or straddled over a chair out by the swimming pool. If you have that kind of camera, you can even photograph them under water if you care to risk getting yourself 'snuffed'.

NOTE: Mike was my best friend and I loved him. The horror of killing him was the sexiest idea I could imagine. He'd trust me all the way through to the end. I suggested the pool and Stan thought that was a good idea . . . He was screaming. Stan put a finger up Mike's nose and pushed it hard to one side, breaking the nose . . . Then we pushed him underwater. We held him there and he struggled. Soon he was still. I carried him to the pool deck and kissed his dead mouth and put my cock up his cool quiet ass again and again.

Mike Robarts,
'Pages from a porno novel I wrote at sixteen',
Gay Sunshine

Greek gods at the filling station with their coveralls open all the way down to their bush of smoky pubic hair. Greek gods disguised as carhops and bellhops and shortorder cooks. Greek gods as sailors in skintight tailormades or summer whites, Army Navy Air Force Marines, firemen forestrangers garbagemen and . . . ye gods! . . . truckers brakemen crane operators even cops: plumbers painters postmen messengerboys movers or call your favourite male madame to order an Apollo. Or you may choose to cruise the laundromats where vagrant Western Apollos can often be found naked, wearing only their cowboy hats and boots as they wash out their levis.

When I stumbled ashore on Apollo's island, I nearly ran into an ugly mob of primitive Christian iconoclasts chanting their hymns of hate in Latin as they wound their way through the burnt-out streets of Delos down to the little port where they boarded their stinking fishing boats to raise the Sign of the Cross on their fish-stained sails. The Romans crucified thousands of criminals like these vandals, lining the Via Appia Antica with them, right in front of the villas of the movie stars. 'By Jesus H. Christ on the Cross,' says Peter the fisherman, 'that's the end of them indecent old heathen gods, brethren. We've busted the last of them.'

All of the hundreds of monumental male members in erection on the island have been mutilated and smashed. The avenue of marble lions, who were said to roar when a virgin boy passed, has been overturned. The alleys lined with intimate phallic shrines, with space for only two lovers at a time to worship the male member, have been put to the torch. Sex was THE big deal on Delos, male sex. The roofless temples open to the Clear Light of Attica, the Real Thing! enshrined giant phalluses as tall as a man pointing to Helios, the Sun, like the gnomons of sundials casting no shadow at high noon. Present Time Forever, loaded and ready to fire off a salvo of sperm in honour of the Sun. An orgasm is the little death and rebirth, out of Time and back into Time again. The great trick, as I see it from where I stand, is not to be born back into the same Time, not to be born back again at all. When you do, you have lost the time you were 'out', be it only a femtosecond, and this is 10^{-15} or a mere 1/1,000,000,000,000,000th of a second. Whew! You can never regain it unless at the moment in question you manage to slip into that aspect of the godhead you are knowing and stay there, becoming immortal, the god Himself. This is what I am about to attempt.

There remains almost no time at all for me to cleanse myself ritually, washing off the blue scum of Mictasol on my skin. I hurry on in search of Apollo's pond and when I get there I see that the colonnade of elegant marble columns around the little spa has been smashed. The marble massage parlours and the dressing rooms for changing your image when you come here on a pilgrimage have been desecrated with human filth. Where is the statue of the beautiful young god by Phidias who sculpted the Parthenon? Searching through the rubble I find him headless in a broom closet and upside down. His arms have been broken off at the shoulder and his legs just below his dimpled knees. His penis, which was attached by a plug into the torso above the carved testicles, has been pulled out by the roots and carried off by some sneaky closet queen of a Christian who shoved it up his ass to masturbate under his filthy peasant smock.

I have received instruction. I know what I must do. I must ejaculate on the god's broken member to bring him back to the point where I can become the god myself in the flashbulb of orgasm. To become one with him I must anoint him with my very last splash of sperm. I am in erection and hot with excitement when a deathly chill falls on me. A cloud seems to come sliding between me and the sun. Is someone approaching or is it a cold blast of alien thinking? A giant vampire bat is attacking me. Is my chance at the godhead going to be snatched away from me at this last fraction of a second? Am I going to be born again in one of those waiting womb-traps my guru warned me against? Through the static which builds up in the darkening air I hear the worst news in the world for me in my condition, the voice of a woman, the ugliest sound in the world.

'Ma Ma Ma!' she is screaming, 'Me Me Me!'

I'd know that voice anywhere and I know all about her, all all all! Everything is lost.

She had a long story behind her, of course. She was a former sacred prostitute from the Temple at Baalbek where she had been the cast-off mistress of the Director, Himself. She thought she had an Eternal Sinecure in the Sacred Grove but when, after a tiff with the Chairperson in charge of the Sacred Secretarial Pool, she tossed in her resignation, not thinking for a moment they would accept it, they did. She was dumbo, dumbfounded. Then began screaming so loud she lost her voice. So she was out of a job. No longer could she lead the sacred chorus of secretaries in the official orgy called by various names: *Ra on the Ramparts, Baal in the Bathtub, Jehovah in Jail, Jesus in a Jumpsuit, etcetera*, during which she took on all the gods one after another, all all all! For years, she carried on around the convent as if there was no other sacred prostitute but her could carry out these Special Rites. She was not universally loved in the industry. They jumped on her resignation to write her off on ILWP, indefinite leave without pay. That is why she finds herself on the highseas in the hold of a trampship bound for Delos with a cargo of eunuchs.

She'd show them! . . . those male chauvinist pigs who took her towel concession away from her without compensation, she'd show them and how! Why, this beautiful big blond boy who speaks no more Greek than a newborn babe, he is hers! She found him. She can make anything she wants out of him . . . a dentist . . . a doctor . . . a poet painter sculptor architect, an artist . . . or a big business tycoon with a temple behind him to take in the cash . . . he'll found a new religion . . . her son . . . her only beloved son . . . her lover . . . her god! Yes, why not make him a god, the new Number One God. Youth and beauty, that always sells. An athlete . . . a racing driver running races with the sun . . . a basketball player who tosses the sun through the hoop every day forever . . . he always wins his match against darkness . . . oh, she is only dreaming but she knows the ropes. The *dea ex machina*, she knows how it is done. Not for nothing has she given the best years of her life to the Temple and seen the huge prices they pay for mere marble images of the gods. She'll show them! She'll show them a real god in flesh and blood, her baby. You just have to take one look at him to see he has the godhead as all the best male babies do. The perfect model. You can see at a glance he photographs divinely. His image will take over the world market and sell anything from baby food to basketball boots. And she will be behind him all the way. Her creation. She always knew she was an artiste and here she has the raw material in front of her. Come on! Let's go! Hit the trail in our Apollo Day-glo hi-tops.

Face facts. He is not the least teensy weensy little bit grateful for all that I've done for him and that's that. I taught him to talk. I taught him the language. I brought him up. I made him a star. And he treats me like dirt. How do you like that? Here I paid for everything for years and years, absolutely everything from the time he was born. And then one day I said to myself: enough is enough! What has he done for me, lately . . . or ever? Tell me that. I am not just his manager. I am his mother. I deserve more respect. More respect and more gratitude, don't you think? After all that I've done for him. What do you think? Hmm? As soon as I set eyes on him I knew he had star quality, just like that. I knew he could play all the parts, not the heavies but the heroes; all the football and basketball heroes from here to eternity, all the blond blue-eyed halfwitted cowboys who triumph over the beetle-browed heavies which is what I *really* like . . . but never mind, I made *my* choice and *he's* got to pay for it. This thing has gone on long enough. All these beachboys who become stars are alike: they don't even know the meaning of the word gratitude, do they? You know he threatened to sue me over that part I got him in the Holy Land picture where he ended up crucified. After all, he'd played the role before in that earlier Syrian production about Attis but that was when he was younger and not such a big star. I wrote all his scripts. Natch. That was part of our contract right from the start.

'You're a star but I'll make you into something more, since you are dead. I'll make you a god. Immortal!' the lady said.

At that price, he had to go along with her. It was an offer he could not refuse.

The first thing she did was to whip out her cloak of invisibility and toss it over his nakedness. 'No goddamned little pipsqueak of a queer Curator is going to come cruising in Greece and grab *this* one away from me!' she mutters fiercely. This will be a lesson to them with their Museum stuffed full of dead gods. She'll show them. She'll come up with a live one. '*Me Me Me! Ma Ma Ma! Me Ma! Me Ma! M A M A M A!*' she keeps chanting as she gives him a rubdown and a bit of unethical massage with her invisible cloak. 'I knew it, I knew it,' she keeps saying to herself, 'the Scientologists are right every time. All you have to do is to say to yourself with purposeful intent: "There is always one for me!" . . . and you'll get it. As I scrambled off that miserable little scum boat to land here in Delos, I kept

saying to myself that I was going to come across something big
. . . and just look at this one! Ten inches if it isn't eleven or
twelve and as hard as marble.'

'Yes yes yes,' she hisses between her teeth which seem to
have sprouted back into her mouth, making it a little harder to
give him head. The thought shoots through her mind: with a
prick as big as this, Deep Throat would be truly impossible, or
heavenly thought!, you could choke to death on it. What is so
great is that as she moulds his magnificent prick in the folds of
her cloak, visibly her hands are getting younger. At the touch
of him, her trembling old knotted hands are unfolding from
the claws they have been for so long. Her nails are blooming
up rosy and tapering. She can see the liver spots flee from the
backs of her hands as the knotted blue veins sink back into the
plump flesh beneath her soft skin. Her tits are filling up, too,
swelling up with nipples erect as she rubs them over his deep
chest with pectoral muscles so pronounced they stick out like
breasts on him. She always was hot for really great pecs; all the
gods got them. She knew. Back in the Sacred Grove, she had
taken on all of them. But this one is something else again. Her
whole pelvic basin feels full of him.

This is exactly what she always wanted: a man without a
head, an invisible man with the biggest prick in the world and
enough ass to swing it. Not that he is swinging anything. He is
just standing there like a statue with her cloak wound around
his head so she won't feel ashamed of anything she is doing to
him. This is a new sensation for her and she loves it. She has
become a Virgin. After all those thousands of men and gods
she laid back in all the temples she worked for, she has finally
pulled the fastest trick of them all. She has become a Virgin.
As she climbs him with her arms wound around his neck and
her thighs locked around his hips and his waist as she mounts
him and rides him, she finds her voice coming back. Her
thighs are splitting apart. Her head whirls because the head of
his penis is so deep in the neck of her womb. She loses all
sense of direction as she gives birth to him. She tears the caul
of her cloak off his head to find his mouth, kissing him fiercely

as she comes to orgasm while chewing his bee-stung lower lip till it bleeds. He is dying. She is being born again. She is dying. He is being reborn as the blood flows from him. From her. From her womb. He is dying in the West. She is rising in the East. She is setting as he rises again in the East, ever more glorious. He is still wrapped in his caul in the tomb of her womb and his winding sheet is tearing. Tearing her apart, wailing. He is rising from his tomb with the sheet falling away from his naked body above which is shining his godhead like a nimbus around the sun over which a cloud is passing. She is the cloud. Her cloak is the cloud with all the stars and the crescent moon caught in it. Her feet are firmly planted on the crescent of the young May moon. She is alone. She is the sole Queen of Heaven.

Her first mistake was the statue. Women cannot resist making replicas, multiples. It is their trade. The very first idea that came into her head was to have a plaster cast made of him by a Greek sculptor she knew from the Temple who was spending the summer on the nearby island of Mykonos. With her rather skimpy cloak of invisibility wrapped around both of them, she herded him on to the tourist ferry because neither of them had the penny to pay Charon the Boatman. The Meltemi was blowing and the passage was rough. Seasick summer visitors were surprised to see a heroic naked arm or classical thigh suddenly appear in their midst every time the wind whipped her cloak off him. Even more surprised to be showered with his vomit.

It is the cocktail hour, the blue hour when they land on Mykonos. Chic summer people are sipping their ouzos around tables set out on the cobbled portside terraces of tourist cafés. She cannot hold him back. He breaks away from her to snatch drinks left and right from the tourists, swilling them down right under their noses, grabbing others off trays before the waiters can serve them. He is drunk, hopelessly drunk and affectionate all of a sudden with one hand on her ass. She steers him up a whitewashed cobblestone alley leading to the sculptor's studio deep in the maze of crooked pedestrian passages. In summer, this area is heavily infested with package-tour tourists. No danger from them, however. What she feared most was an encounter with some horrible Hippy or Harpy or Homo so she kept him on a pretty short leash until they got to the sculptor's blue-painted door, a low door set deep in a whitewashed wall.

She just happened to catch the sculptor with a batch of fresh plaster on his hands. The Greek sculptor dropped whatever it was he was doing when he saw the naked frame on her find. His chin dropped when she whipped her cloak off me and let it bounce up and down there where she hung it on my erection, my colossal, my godlike erection. As she plucked it off my prick with a ladylike gesture, I flipped when the Greek grabbed for the glycerine to anoint it. I became harder than marble and could have stayed that way forever if only she hadn't started doing her hoochie-coochie temple dance, makes my blood run cold. I began to lose my erection, go soft and droopy.

'Hey, cut that out!' cried the sculptor. 'Can't you see you're making him lose his hard-on. I'll have to do this over again. Here, you,' he addressed me, 'here's some beefcake to freshen you up. It's a porn publication from Denmark called *Greek Gods*. You see,' he went on, turning to her, 'that's what excites him, his own image. I could pose him for Narcissus, too.'

'No no no!' she cried. 'He is Apollo! I just gave birth to him on the island of Delos. I work for the Museum. I'M A CURATOR! I should know.'

'OK, Apollo it is, but I'm only going to take a cast of what he's got between his legs. The rest of his features are purely classical blond god's features and chassis. You can pick them up in any model agency for cheap.'

Goddammit! Goddammitohell! she keeps saying over and over to herself just under the breath: Why the fucking hell don't I still have my trusty old Canon FT? These are just the colour pics I could sell to *Playgirl* for a big spread around the centrefold. Just think of it! I could clean up. Why, with this

Divine Light, I could shoot him directly in Ektachrome from way over here on the far side of this studio with my 200 mm lens, almost. I could squeeze it down to a real fast speed like ... and she finds herself squeezing her dry old thighs together at the mere thought of it. Image-making always brings on this fever. Her eyes roll back in her head and fog over with equal parts of pain and pleasure. Her head is swimming. She finds herself clamping her bony old thighs tighter and tighter together because some sticky substance is oozing down her legs. Can this be? What is it? Is she going to be sick to her stomach or what? What the hell is happening here, anyway? Nothing even remotely like this ever happened to her with any of the hundreds or thousands of pilgrims she serviced back in the Temple or out in the Sacred Grove. Never.

The sculptor is peeling the just-hardened plaster off the boy's prick with care, exquisite care. She simply can't bear it! The Greek sculptor is wildly excited himself, as she can plainly see. His own cock is poking straight out in front of him under his spotted sculptor's smock, but it is not nearly as big as her hero's. Oh no! Now, he and he alone is her baby, her beauty, her god. But what in the god's name is happening to her? Is she having the very first orgasm of her life or is she having an attack of the squitters? Is she coming down with the collywobbles, the shits, dysentery, or is she about to relive one of those hundreds of abortions she used to give herself in the past with a fork in the communal kitchens of the Temple? Or ... oh, ye gods! ... is she about to give birth, not to just this one beautiful boy but to all of the many millions of multiples she can have made of his image, his immortal reflection, his rampant erection, now that the sculptor has made a mould of it?

But this greedy Greek sculptor simply does not see it her way. Oh no, not at all!

'This creation is mine,' he states flatly, 'all mine and nobody else's. It is my work,' he insists, 'my creation, my masterpiece. Nobody else but me could make this. It is mine and I am going to sign it. I can't give it or loan it or lease it to you because I am under exclusive contract to Ionas.'

'And who the hell is Ionas?' she screams.

'You mean to say you never heard of Ionas? He's my dealer.'

'No.'

'Ionas of Immortal Images Inc.? IIII?'

'That sounds to me like one more male chauvinist pig, typically egotistical. I'll bet he's a fag. Your Ionas is never going to get his filthy paws on my golden boy here. I'll see to that.'

'But Ionas will see to it that this statue of mine gets into the Museum!'

'The Museum?' she snorts. 'I'll see to it that he gets into *the Temple*! Into the Temple as a god with an altar of his very own. I'm sorry we wasted your time. I've just had a *much* better idea. We don't want your old statue. We don't need it, thank you very much. He is going to have a magnificent altar right in the middle of the Temple and there will be nothing on it. No sculpture. No image. Nothing. How do you like that? Just candles and flowers and no statue at all. I'm going to make him the Invisible God.'

And with that she picks up a hammer to smash the Greek sculptor's hardening plaster cast. He grabs her arm. She sinks her teeth into his hand. He gives her a smashing backhand across the face. She kicks his shins. He tries to wrist-wrestle the hammer out of her hand. The hammer drops, smashing the cast. She lets out a yell of triumph. He lets out a yell of rage and despair. Our beautiful young hero, the subject and the object of this titanic struggle, taking advantage of this dichotomy, snatches up her invisible cloak, wrapping it around him as he dashes out the door. Outside in the narrow white-washed alley, he gets his bearing through the maze of Mykonos streets leading down to the port where a sponge fisherman is casting off. One great flying leap lands him aboard with her skimpy invisible cloak fluttering out behind him.

Rich Athenian summer visitors looking up from their back-gammon boards outside the portside cafés and several Scandinavian tourists loitering along the jetty saw a naked golden

124

godlike form with a bathing-suit mark of white ass flash through the air just as a great forked bolt of lightning split the Cycladic sky. The light went out like a total eclipse as the Meltemi hit the little ship and sank it just outside the harbour.

'Baby baby bay-bee!' she is cooing over him. 'Boyoboyoboyoboyo BOY! Have I ever got me a live one! Just look at this prick on him. Isn't that just too cute ... googoogoo! Gimme that cute thing of yours, pronto! Gimme gimmee gimmeeeE! Oooo, he's ticklish ... see how he's grinning. Mamamama-maA! I'm your Mother, say Mamma ... no don't pull away like that. You can't getta getta gettaway from me. I am your Mother and I've gotcha gotcha cotcha!'

She is all dolled up in her desert drag, her outfit for archaeological expeditions and digs, the colours of dust and shadow. A khaki safari suit from Nieman Marcus and a Whitehunter's hat from Abercrombie and Fitch with a Somali leopardskin band around it. She is all wrapped up in dirty old burnouses and spotted flowing veils she picked up on her travels. She is veiled up to her Rayban shades. You cannot really be sure there is a face in there. Her age? You can't tell in southern California. There are some plenty weird old witches flying along the freeways on their wheels with their metal wings spread to swoop down on innocent hitch-hikers or dumb truckdrivers. They snip off their balls with nail-scissors. 'Stop that!' they scream in mock alarm at the mere male they have picked up. 'Stop rubbing your crotch like that! Are you trying to seduce me, little man? Show me that thing of yours. Pah! You think something as small as that interests me?'

He groans because he has been through all this scene before, only too often. Then, she suddenly turns coy, begins panting that she really wants him ... needs him. 'Just let me hold that big old thing of yours while I park this heap in this dark alley.' And she pulls out her ...

'No no no,' he groans, 'let's not go through all that again!'

'But I love you,' she coos. 'I'm your Mother. I loves ya. Ya gotta believe me, I really do, *reeelly*!'

'Not here,' he protests, 'it's too public. Besides, you're not supposed to handle the exhibits.'

'But I'm a Curator,' she informed him, 'and I have every right to handle the exhibits and to catalogue them. This is my business. Here, give me that thing of yours. I'll take care of it. I'll have a plaster cast made and I'll put it in the Museum. Won't *you* be flattered, Buster. I'll make you immortal. Future generations of women will come to admire your mould when there are no more men left on earth. This is your chance, you better take it. You need me, Big Boy, for this operation. Believe me. I loves ya, besides, and ya needs me. Without me and my womb there is no way of making multiples out of moulds, ya hear me? Already, you are as superfluous as the dinosaur but your Mother loves you, you better believe me.'

'Hey, wait a minute, lady! If you are my mother, I don't think we are supposed to be doing this thing together. That's incest.'

'Let's just say I'm your Old Lady. You make me feel so maternal, protective, I'll call you my baby. I've always wanted a man like that, a big *baybee*! A man with a beautiful body and no head just like you when I found you. And, besides, I'm a Curator and you'll be the Find of the Century! When I propose you to the Trustees, they'll reinstate me.'

'Reinstate you? You mean you're not really attached to the Museum, right now? They fired you?'

'You can't fire me, Buster, nobody can. I resigned. I meant it to be a lesson to them. What could they do without me? I was in charge of Reproduction and Replicas. Who else can do that for them? Some little faggot with a sex change? Don't make me laugh. They need me . . . me me ME and Me only, you hear me? The fools did pretend to accept my resignation but they can't get away with that. They can't do a thing without me me ME! I'll be back in charge, soon. And I'll take you with me.'

'I don't think they need *me*. You said that yourself, just now, and you've completely convinced me, completely. I can't reproduce all alone, as you know very well, but you, you can get cracking on that test tube of sperm without me.

Without me, you hear me? Without *me*. Alone is the operative word and I wish you the best. I really do. I'll be glad to go, now, and turn the whole operation over to you, believe me. Good luck and goodbye. *Ave atque vale!*'

'Oh, very well,' she huffs, 'if that's the way you want it, I give up. You do just whatever . . . *sob!* . . . your little heart desires . . . you men always do. You know you rule me. You rule over me with that rod of yours.'

'Me? *Me* rule *you*? I hope not. You are utterly free to do as you will. Goodbye, I'm going thataway. You know which way it is back to the Beat Hotel in the Latin Quarter on the Left Bank of Paris?'

'Well, if you don't want to play . . .'

'I don't! I'm tired and I want to get back to my hotel. Can you tell me . . . ?'

'Yes, I can but, before I tell you which way it is, can I take a few pictures? I've got one roll of Kodacolor II film left in my camera and I'd like to have something to remember you by. After all, you are my idol. I'll have a big blow-up print made and I'll put it in my shrine beside my photo of Valentino and then I'll take my sleeping pills on my knees in front of it, just like I did for him.'

'You really did that? It's so corny! What an old-fashioned fan story!'

'Yes,' she breathes, but she is already leaping about like Bruce Lee taking pictures of him at a fast speed because there is still that Divine Light hovering over him. She can squeeze it down to one in a thousand. Not very fast for those who deal in, even, microseconds.

NOTE: One microsecond is 10^{-6} or: one in 1,000,000th part of a second.

She is hopping about like a paparazzi, snatching his image away from him by the millisecond.

NOTE: A millisecond is 10^{-3} or: one in 1,000th part of a second. Time enough.

She is peeling layer after layer, skin after skin off his onion of karma, snatching him away while leaving him there. And other minor magics.

'No more pictures! That's enough! Put that camera away. Just tell me, which way is it back to the Hip Hotel in Paris on the Left Bank in the Latin Quarter? Which way is it back to the Beat ... uh ... I mean the Bardo?'

'Oh, taking nude pictures of you just thrills me! I simply know I can sell this packet to *Playgirl* for a centrefold and six or eight pages ... or maybe more! ... the whole issue ... the whole book, as they call it. There, just look straight at me ... look at the birdie I have down here in my nest of pubic hair. Just look at me ... I'm lovely! See, I don't wear a bra and I don't wear a girdle ... my Girdle of Venus, I mean. I don't need to. Oh, Mr Apollo, couldn't you get just a little wee bit more ... what the girls back in the office call ... "imminent turgescence" ... into that big prick of yours? Look into the camera. Looka me! Doesn't that make it come bigger? Oh, I'm getting my rocks off on you. I may be old but I'm still desirable, ain't I?'

'Look lady, all I wanna know is what way it is back to the Latin Quarter.'

'There, I've finished. I've almost finished my roll and I've had my orgasm. You can go now. You are dismissed.'

'Which way is it to the Latin Quarter?' he whines like a schoolboy.

'Over that way, I guess. You see those long-haired hippies coming back from the Far Eastern Section? They're taking the short-cut through the old French ex-colonies where heroin is still being pushed. All you have to do is cross the bridge over the Rangoon River or the Seine and you are in the Place Saint-Michel where they straggle in from Kathmandu with chains of buffalo ivory skulls around their necks, sleeping on the floor of the Shakespeare and Co. bookshop. Can I take one last picture? By the way, I think you should see a doctor. Get a check-up, y'know?'

CHAPTER FOUR
FLOOR FOUR
WEEK FOUR
ROOM 22

'Hi, Doc!' I greet old Adam when he drops in on his second visit to Room Twenty-two. 'I can hear people out there on the stairs. What floor is this that I'm on anyway?'

'It depends on the way you count floors, old man,' he comes back, very British. 'If you count them the American way, this is the fourth floor, but almost anywhere else it's only the third. Like here in the Bardo, for instance.'

'I'm an American and I want things counted the American way,' I growl. 'You understand me, oldboy oldboyo? This is the Fourth Floor and I've got to get out of here. This place is terrible. It stinks. If this is a hospital bed in a private room, then the Crimean War must still be going on. Send me in Sister Florence Nightingale.'

'Shush!' he murmured. 'She's the matron now and she's running the old Bardo like a barracks. I'm scared stiff of her. She's taken over from Madame Rachou, you know. You won't be seeing *her* around here for a while.'

'Why, what happened?'

'They flew Madame Rachou over to inaugurate their new installation in the Beat Museum in Palmdale, good old Palmdale-on-the-Bulge in Sunny Southern California.'

'No!' I cried. 'No! You've got to be joking. They can't *do* that! They can't inaugurate anything out there without me ... me me ME! Without me, the Museum doesn't even exist. It's all my invention, mine mine mine!'

'Ah yes, but,' he says, 'since your accident ... Here, let's just take a look at those legs of yours. We can't have a nasty old infection setting in, can we?'

'Ach, who cares anymore! I don't feel them, can't even see

them since you've got me here blind and in total restraint, in this totally miserable sort of sub-Samuel Beckett situation. But how about my colostomy? How am I going to handle my bowel movements? Tell me that.'

'No problem. We've got you on a fibre-free diet and you may not be having all that many more bowel movements, anyway. But, just in case you do, we'll run a long plastic sleeve out between the bars on your interior window, here, from your stoma straight down into the Turkish toilet on the turn in the stairs. That'll fix it. I'll have Violet come down from upstairs to help you. She loves giving enemas.'

'You don't mean Doc Benway's nutty nurse, do you? That unlicensed blue-assed baboon who sniffed up all his cocaine on him?'

'I'll not have one word said against Violet,' he sniffed. 'Violet is the only woman I ever really loved.'

'You, too?' I laughed. 'And how about Eva?'

'Dr Eva is my wife and that's different,' he replied rather stiffly.

'Can Violet really come downstairs? I didn't know anyone could come back down once they'd made it up there to those upper floors of the Bardo.'

'Only animals. Our popstar son, Mickey Monkey, scampers all over the old hotel, you know. Or he used to. And Violet. You should see old Violet come tearing down after him with her big old syringe at the ready when he goes on a rampage and comes swarming downstairs in a rage ready to kill our other son, his brother Abel. Violet cools him out with a shot of Lithium. That does it. She's saved Abel's life several times over. Eva and I are both very grateful.'

'And how old is Abel?'

'Thirteen. They're both thirteen, born only a few minutes apart in good old Benway's Maternity Mansion, that's what he called it. Ah, our salad days! We squatted this whole row of broken-down boarded-up Victorian mansions in the East End of London. We ran the only clinic in the world at that time with psychiatric services for over-privileged primates. You know, over-liberated apes, broken-down victims of laboratory experiments, hysterical female chimps punching out heart-rending messages in Yerkish on imaginary computers: *"Help! Help!"* or: *"Please Machine Tickle Lana"*. Schizoid males simultaneously signing out contradictory sentences in AMSLAN, American Sign Language, which the deaf can read if they speak English, and UKSLAN which Americans can't always quite catch if it's spoken quickly. AMSLAN with the right hand and UKSLAN with the left. Most disturbing. Jason the Astronaut, our pioneer space ape, died in our arms. Very touching. We all learned a lot. When Eva and Violet gave birth less than an hour apart the same day, we decided to bring the boys up as twins. Violet, oddly enough, wanted to have nothing to do with either of them so it was Eva's decision to breast feed them both. Naturally enough, we christened them Cain and Abel.'

'That may not have been entirely wise.'

'No, but a love–hate relationship was bound to develop between them. As they grew up, of course, it grew worse. Today, Abel is barely adolescent while Cain, whose record company changed his name to Mickey Monkey, is getting quite a few grey hairs here and there. His pubic hair is going quite white but he dyes it because of his groupies.'

'Did I understand you to say you had them both christened as Christians?'

'Why not? I baptized them both myself, personally. I'm a sort of a priest, you know, as well as a medical doctor, and so is Eva. We've got our certificates from the same mail order institute out in California. Mickey's baptism is good, it holds water, Holy Water. Even the Catholics have to admit it. Yes, poor old Mickey was baptized and all that, but it doesn't make him a human, of course, not legally and that's his big beef. He has an amazing IQ and that drove him insane. With his bread and his fans, if he had been born in the States he could have made it to President. If you can remember that far back, Burroughs nominated him at the Democratic Convention in Chicago. He wrote a piece for *Esquire* about it called "The Coming of the Purple-Assed Better One". It didn't work.'

'Does Mickey really have a purple ass?'

'No, blue. But he made enough money with his music to buy the White House itself and he knows it. I don't want to sound rude, but he was earning enough money to buy your Museum of Museums right out from under you if his career had only gone on long enough.'

'Really? You amaze me. And where has all that money gone, may I ask?'

'To the taxman, mostly. The rest went into a trust.'

'In his own name, I trust. What is his own name, by the way, his real name?'

'His mother has never wanted to talk. Good old Violet, she's far too professional, even though she never really took the Hypocritic Oath. We don't even know who his biological father was.'

'Not Benway? Not you?'

'Come off it! You know that's genetically impossible, or was until very recently.'

'That's just what I mean.'

'Violet never names names.'

'So, what's his status?'

'Now, right now? He's a chattel. Eva and I own him jointly. He may have made the greatest fortune in rock history but he can't own a dime. We put the trust in Abel's name as long as he's still a minor. There's legislation to protect a child star so he sings soprano with the band. That's another reason Mickey wants to kill him, I guess.'

'Don't you let Mickey have any money at all?'

'For a while we let him play with his money in public. It was good business and great publicity when he showered his fans at a concert with thunderstorms of folding money blowing out over the crowds, causing riots. Dollar bills and even twenties and fifties or even hundreds used to drift down over his frenzied fans but we had to put a stop to that when so many were injured that the stretcher brigades couldn't carry them off. Eventually, because we couldn't stop him from throwing the money away, we put him on Lithium.'

'Yeah, Lithium. The Family put me on Lithium, too, when they felt I was spending too much money on my Museum. Is that what Lithium does?'

'Absolutely, the Saudi Arabians found it worked on spendthrift young princes who were spending too much on cocaine. Mickey was giving us plenty of trouble on that score, too, so we cooled him out. It made another monkey of him.'

'And cooled him out for good into the bargain, eh?'

'Oh, I don't know. You may hear him rampaging up and down the stairs under your window any day now.'

'Looking to score for some coke?'

'I'd be surprised if there was any coke in the Bardo. The Tibetans don't like it. Don't approve. It isn't really their style.'

'I wonder why. If the coca bush grows up on the Altiplano of Chile it ought to do well in Tibet.'

'Say, that's a great idea. I'll have to ask Benway, he's been to Bolivia to score.'

'If I were you, I'd check with the Tibetans first. By the way, I hear Mickey Monkey is writing his memoirs.'

'If he is, that's another secret he's keeping from me. He can't write. I don't mean he can't write well. I mean he can't write, period. Never learned. He can read well enough to get the drift of a contract but he prefers to have it read aloud to him. Something the matter with his eyes. He can't read the small print.'

'Neither could I, not even when I had my eyesight. All that small print got me into plenty of trouble.'

'Him, too. He can write his own name on the dotted line but that's about it. Just never got the knack of it manually, that's all. He uses the typewriter and his computers whereas his brother Abel can't read OR write. We brought them both up permissively according to Dr Spock, and Abel got spocked worse. No repressive disciplines of any kind, not even potty training. The result is that our Abel at the age of thirteen still doesn't know how to use the toilet alone while his twin brother Cain is getting on into late middle age for a monkey.

However, they are both absolute geniuses on the most sophisticated software. It helps.'

'That's how Mickey learned to communicate in the first place, wasn't it, with computers?'

'At Georgia Tech, of all places. We wanted them both to learn Yerkish, the first interprimate language invented by the good Dr Yerkes, an old pal of Benway's, of course.'

'But how did Mickey get into pop music?'

'That was easy, inevitable, why not? We took them both to a concert of the Strolling Ruins. Abel put his fingers in his ears and screamed so we knew he'd be the singer while Mickey, who was still known as Cain, of course raised bloody hell by jumping right up on to the stage and taking over the show. He simply flattened the drumsets and swung through the whole setup, destroying more electronic equipment than anyone else in pop history to the utter delight of those millions of young people who became his fanatic fans forever. There are still Mickey Monkey Memorials going up all over the globe.'

'I suppose it all went to his head.'

'Oh, it did, my dear, he became absolutely impossible to live with because the irony of his situation made him so bitter, so very bitter. There he was with the world at his feet, so to speak, yet he couldn't open a bank account in his own name even though all those millions came pouring in. When he got behind a wheel, he drove like a maniac but he couldn't get a driving licence, let alone a passport or even a dog licence, and he really desperately wanted to own a dog, own something anything anybody at all! Considering some of the bitches who were after him for his money, it was just as well he couldn't get married. He ran up huge bills in bars, treating everybody, drinking straight bourbon with beer chasers, boilermakers. One time in Paris, he trashed the Ritz bar.'

'Me, too. Those are real killers. I used to drink them myself when I was, ah, younger. I remember hearing he was the first to use computers on his synthesizers. Is that true?'

'That's what did it. Made him Numero Uno on all the charts worldwide overnight. Why, his first gold . . .'

'Yeah, I remember: The Monkeyshiners.'

'No, that first platter never made it to gold. He only made it to gold when his record company changed the name of the group to: Mickey Monkey and the Shiners.'

'Yeah, the Shiners made a big hit right away, I remember.'

'Excuse *me*! The Shiners got lost. Mickey Monkey made a colossal hit right away. Overnight, he became the greatest star ever, anywhere. He really blew all their fuses. He was overwhelming, overweening, whatever! He'll be remembered forever.'

'Forever is a long long time. They were always having trouble over their album covers, weren't they? I remember the cover on *Raising Cain*. The feminists really hated that one, didn't they? Wow!'

'Sometimes those women are silly, plain silly. What set them off was those baby pictures of Eva suckling off our two little boys simultaneously. Talk about racism and sexism together! They're sick, those women, crazy, plain crazy.'

'Yeah, I guess you're right. There was nothing, ah, prurient about all that, now was there?'

'Their next cover had Mickey with a big black cigar between his teeth like Groucho, leering down into Eva's deep cleavage. *Forbidden Fruits*, it was called. There was an even bigger hullabaloo about that one. They said he had a hard-on. Of course he did. Mickey always had an erection on stage all the time he was playing, like a bullfighter. That's what made the music so great. Sex. Sex raised its ugly head there while we still had him and Abel in rompers. Of course it raised its ugly head with Abel too but nobody even noticed because his was so small while Mickey already had a good 21 centimetres.'

'How much does that make in inches? I never can remember how you turn centimetres into inches.'

'Never mind. He got a reputation for chasing girls and being very very destructive. Much more than most rock stars, even. That made him even more popular with his peers. I mean humans. For sheer destructiveness, no other animal can beat humans. Mickey made his mark by destroying even more expensive electronic equipment than even The Speedsters.'

'Yeah, they were pretty good. Bad, I mean. Great.'

'Not as great as Mickey because they never really experienced the extreme psychic pain he did, always. The more the money rolled in, the more heavy psychic pain he suffered because no one ever gave him his due as a being. He felt frustrated because the law and society treated him as a minor.'

'Yes, a lot of the kids feel like that, these days.'

'But they don't have the kind of money to throw around he did.'

'Oh, I don't know. Little PG does. Little PG Six. With his kind of bread, he can move Heidelberg Castle to Hoboken, if he wants to.'

'Yeah, but who wants to? Say, who is he, this little PG Six you're always talking about? Who is he, anyway, tell me.'

'Me, as a matter of fact. But go on. You were saying?'

'They grow out of it eventually. They grow up. Mickey grew up even quicker, being a monkey. By the time he was six he was a multi-millionaire many times over. Except behind the Iron Curtain, he'd been everywhere, met everybody. Especially the rich kids of the British nobility who dressed like him and imitated him, trashing everything everywhere. Burning down their own stately homes. Millions tuned in on him and turned out for his concerts. His albums all went from gold to platinum and over. He was living in a dream until he was traumatized by the ugly truth: he could never buy his way into society.'

'Society? You mean he's a snob?'

'Human society. He began hating his money.'

'That happened to Little PG Six, too.'

'There you go again. Who is he?'

'Just a little boy I knew, almost as rich as I was. Never mind. Go on with what you were saying about Mick and his money.'

'As I said, when he found out he couldn't even have a bank account, he began showering the kids with his money. They went wild, especially the rich kids who always go around poor-mouthing people about how they've got no money, dressed in rags and tatters from the top Japanese dress designers.'

'Little PG Six, too.'

'Hundreds of them were trampled to death in the mêlée. Mickey used to have men from the Mint and the Treasury Department come on stage wheeling great stacks of money he'd dump on the stage and set fire to with a flamethrower. Rich kids who were his onstage guests in the Hospitality Area or fellow popstars used to throw themselves into the holocaust to rescue dollar bills singed around the edges. Sometimes they suffered third degree burns. Eva and Violet and I used to have to attend to them. They really cared about that money. Mickey despised them for it. No amount of money could buy what he wanted, what he felt was his due.'

'You mean, human status?'

'No no, not just that. Monkeys don't think in such abstract terms. Only humans do. What Mickey wanted was a driving licence. He wanted the right to race great big noisy 2000cc motorbikes up and down the freeways, snaking in and out of traffic with a blonde on the back of his wheel with her hair streaming out a mile behind her. He wanted to race Lamborghinis up and down the hills behind Monte Carlo, to win the cup at Le Mans or whatever. He wanted a licence to fly his own Presidential jet full of air hostesses. You remember those ads they ran? "Fly Me!" He flew all of them.'

'You mean, he had girls?'

'Did he ever! Of course he had girls, he had groupies galore. Most of them were real dogs but some were only slightly used troupe and group followers. Groupies, I treated a lot of them for herpes and hysteria.'

'There's no cure for them, is there?'

'Not yet but they're working on it. Punctured pussies is what gave me the most trouble. I'm not a surgeon so I had to call in Benway and Violet, his mother.'

'Whose mother? Benway's? You mean to say Violet is Benway's mother and here they've been having this long affair! That's incest.'

'Don't be silly. Violet is Mickey's mother.'

'And who did you say was his father?'

'I didn't. None of your business. You see, some of these reckless girls, these hysterical hussies, used to make Mickey wrap a towel around it before intromission because it's so long and pointy.'

'What is, his prick?'

'Yes, his penis is very long and pointy and sometimes the towel comes off. Sometimes the towel would wind itself off, you see, unwind in the action if you see what I mean and it punctured the uterus. Some of those poor girls never recovered.'

'Oh, come on! Twenty-one centimetres must make about 8½ inches. My own was nearly that big when I could still get it up. Any grown girl would love to take that much cock. Mickey must have more than that.'

'He does. Oh, he does. And it went right on growing. It caused us no end of trouble. What with the girls and the drugs, we were glad when it was over. By that time it had nearly doubled in length.'

'Forty-two centimetres! I can't swallow that. No one could have a dong as long as that. Nobody.'

'Of course not. You're right. Nobody human could or if they do it's a case of elephantiasis and they can't get it up. But he can. Or he could. Mickey Monkey. I should know, it cost us a fortune, a whole lot of money. He didn't give a fuck, not one flying fuck! You can't jail a monkey, not a monkey as rich and famous and well loved as he was. No siree! They tried that on us once in Sydney, Australia. His loyal fans stormed the police station and carried him out in triumph on their shoulders. On the strength of that, I was drummed out of the World Psychiatric Association for having contributed to the delinquency of a minor. Those people are crazy.'

'I always thought so. By the way, how long do you figure I'm going to be laid up here in Room Twenty-three?'

'Twenty-two, Room Twenty-two. A week, a full week. Matron's orders.'

'A full week?' I screech. 'Every day in this dump is a decade.'

'Yes, it can be, certainly. But, you know, I don't think it was wise of you to say that, right out so loud and clear. You see, if that's what you think, that's the way it can be. That may well turn out to be the way it will seem to you, like a seventy-year week, three score and ten, a life sentence.'

And it does. It *is* a life sentence seven decades long, the week that Dr Adam was talking about. I'm living it, dreaming it. After the good doctor's parting shot of heroin, here I lie nodding out as I run my bare hands over my ruined body, this wreck of my rocket I am still locked into after my crash, after my bonedeep burning with cobalt, my operations with their disastrous anaesthetics and my other accidents mishaps misadventures and misdirections, a long life and a glorious one. They say I complain and I do but let's leave that for later. I've had a good, even a great run for my money. I've run through a great deal of life and a great deal of money. I was loved in my time and I loved. I did not love myself, never. Those who do not love themselves are always right. They know best. Those who do love themselves are always wrong.

Old Adam wakes me to say, 'I've got this patient who wants to see you. Ordinarily it's not allowed. The Tibetan real estate agency that runs this whole Bardo chain, and has now for centuries, laid it down once and for all that clients must move through day by day in the order they, the Tibetans, evolved long ago, but since you upset all that by your move to California, one doesn't know anymore.'

'My fault again, eh? Who is this other patient of yours?'

'A French boy with a long windy name who claims you know his aunt or you used to. He says he used to see you at parties in her house in Paris. He says you'll remember him.'

'I've survived a lot of parties in Paris in my day. Who is his aunt?'

It's his great-aunt. She lived for years with a Chinese lady general.'

'Oh, Freddy! Frederica Forshew of Pride's Crossing, Mass.

She married that dithering old Duc de la Farce who was so well named it was no longer a joke. Of course I remember her and her General Hwang. Freddy called her Ondine. What a pair! They got into some terrible scandal and were said to have committed suicide together. I used to run into those two old dykes at my cousin Antonia Longfinger's place. I don't remember any nephew, though, much less a grand-nephew.'

'He very much hopes you'll remember him. He'll be disappointed. He's terribly fragile.'

'Fragile? What does that mean? Is he a Venetian glass nephew?'

'Something like that. He's in analysis with me.'

'So I suppose you have him on Lithium and all those other horrible drugs you give your poor patients. Anti-depressants, psychic regulators you call them. What a grim joke.'

'It's the scientific approach.'

'Approach to what, to turning them into zombies?'

'He used to be overly highspirited, euphoric and extravagant, throwing his money around lavishly, giving it to leftist organizations, terrorists.'

'Ah, yes, those clubs they have for rich kids, instructions in how to shoot your uncle in the knees and all that. I can see how his family wouldn't like it much.'

'They didn't. Lithium for four years seems to have fixed it, as in the case of my spendthrift Saudi Arabian princes I told you about. We hoped it would cure their homosexuality, too, but it didn't.'

'You mean this young man is gay?'

'Amongst other things. He likes women, too, young and old. And the beasts. Yes, the beasties. He's a bit of a sex snob. He's been after Mickey and even old Violet. Both Eva and I have had him in bed.'

'There you go again, Adam, sleeping with your patients. It isn't allowed.'

'There's no one to stop me. It is my work, as Dr Buroon used to say: Das iss mine *vork*! After all, I'm an anti-psychiatrist, am I not?'

'You old scamp! Tell me more about this young man. Is he good-looking?'

'I don't know.'

'What d'ya mean, ya don' know! Here, you've had him in analysis and you've had him in bed and you claim you don't know. Waddya mean ya don' know?'

'I don't. He goes veiled.'

'He goes what?'

'He wears nothing but smelly Adidas running shoes and a veil over his head. Nothing else. That's all. He's uncircumcised. He has a beautiful penis.'

'What? Even in bed he wears this veil?'

'Yes, even in bed. It's a curious case. He's very well built.'

'He does this out of modesty? Fear of kidnapping? I used to have both. I know.'

'He doesn't seem to know why. That's why I'm analysing him. He says it's because he's afraid of blinding people with his beauty. I've called it the Gorgon or the Medusa complex, that's new. I'm going to have it registered in my name by the Psychiatric Society as soon as they reinstate me. He really doesn't like that idea at all. He says the Medusa is a wicked woman who turns a man into stone while he is Apollo the Sungod who blinds people with the brilliance and heat of his beauty. Me, I don't want to know.'

'Maybe he wants to see me because he knows I can't see him.'

'Perhaps. The only one around here who has seen him unveiled is the slimy little terrorist chick he more or less lives with. They've got a duplex, two rooms, Twenty-six and Twenty-seven. He claims he doesn't have sex with her any more and perhaps it's true. She is a remarkably ugly and vulgar little dwarf with a big ass, a nasty tongue and a terrible temper. It amuses him to call her Freddy just like his American aunt. He is always going over the story of how the two of them met over his accident, his two Freddies.'

'Oh, so he had an accident, too.'

'Every one of us here in the Bardo had an accident or we wouldn't be here.'

'And what happened to him?'

'He blew off both his hands while attaching a charge of plastic to a statue, the base of the statue of Etienne Dolet, the Renaissance publisher, to be exact.'

'Why, whatever for?'

'It is practically impossible to elucidate the criminal impulses of the insane and he *is* mad.'

'And you want me to meet this young madman.'

'It is he who wants to meet you. What shall I tell him? I've got to drop over and give him an hour today. You won't meet him?'

'Why should I? But what do you mean, you've got to drop over and give him an hour? I thought the analysand was always supposed to come to the analyst for his hour.'

'Yes, he used to come to our room but since this thing, this affair has gone on between him and Eva, I go over to his room. Besides, he's been making passes at Abel and Eva won't stand for that. I don't dare tell her I've caught young Abel over there more than once stripped down for . . . well, you know what I mean.'

'No, do I?' I asked rather archly.

'Foutaise explains to me very gently and very patiently that he is teaching the boy martial arts according to a system he calls *Ki no Michi*, very special. The aikido type exercises must be practised in the nude to put the neophyte in a total risk situation, the loss of his balls. At that he whips out a Japanese sabre of the sort they commit hara-kiri with in Japanese movies and whistles it over my head so close that he gave me this flat-top haircut with a shower of chopped hairs falling into my eyes and down the back of my neck. I was so taken by surprise that I didn't even have time to blink let alone flinch away from the blow which might have been fatal. I was rather proud of myself and so was Abel.'

'So am I.'

'So was he. I think he's falling in love with me as all my analysands do.'

'Not me.'

'No, not you. You're incapable of falling in love with any-body because you don't even love yourself,' he snapped as he left.

Then I heard my door slam shut so hard that I laughed. My good doctor left in one hell of a huff. In my book, that could mean only one thing: he's madly in love with me, poor old washed-up me, held here in total restraint. I laughed out loud for the first time since I found myself here in Tomb Twenty-two of the Bardo. It is absurd. He has fallen in love with me when what he meant to happen was that I would fall in love with him. So, I thought to myself, death is just as ridiculous as life, is it. I laughed until I almost choked.

Sinking back into my rotten old memories of love, I found myself once again in that Paris I discovered or was thrust into when I showed up at my great-cousin Antonia's historic town house on the Seine, Number One Paris, the oldest private resi-dence in the city, she always claimed. I was fresh out of my ex-pensive English public school, outfitted on credit by the school tailor with six lounge suits and two dinner jackets but no tails and not a penny to my troublesome name which was, according to the newspapers, the Richest Little Boy in the World. Who would believe that I had only 15 dollars a month? Cousin Antonia Longfinger did because she knew all about the Longfinger Legacy and our mutual ancestor's infamous will by which I could be utterly disinherited because my mother sent me to this Catholic school and then OD'd on us. Antonia took me in and gave me a superb bachelor flat on her top floor, high under her many-gabled roof with a flowering terrace overlooking the Seine and Notre Dame right across from us. Her handsome housekeeper was a Scots gentle-woman in reduced circumstances who adored me. At the age of eighteen, I made the most of it. Lady Fiona used to have the kitchen send me up delicious meals with more than enough caviar and champagne to have my own guests whenever I wanted. I gave little parties for any young people I could find in this strange household of old women.

Antonia entertained lavishly, mainly women. She had her

own Day in the week when she received hordes of people, mainly women. Her day was Friday, no, Friday was Clifford Barney's Day when she, too, received mainly women. All the Great Ladies of Paris had their days of the week when they held their salons but Cousin Antonia's Day was the most exclusive because she was the Vicar General of the Lesbians. She received the faithful of her peculiar parish in a very impressively lofty Gothic great hall which had been the chapel of Joan of Arc, the Maid of Orleans, herself, in person. Antonia presided over these receptions like the Mother Superior of a very fashionable convent. Pilgrims were permitted once a year, tourists never. Only the chosen few were ever invited to stay on for the party after the party to participate in the very private ceremonies which took place there, no men ever admitted. All the highest ranking Gurls in the world passed through Antonia's hands, from royal queens-in-exile off Balkan thrones to reigning and retired queens from Hollywood. The house was so huge and so hospitable that a number of adepts moved in to become her permanent court.

I rarely went out of the house except when I had to because of this queer-looking character who followed me through the streets of Paris wherever I went. Night and day, he lurked in this sinister alley called Chienlit Street which ran up from the river past the front door of Antonia's house. As soon as I ever stepped out into this street, he would loom up out of the shadows to follow me to the Sorbonne for instance. I had to go there to take a course in 'La Civilisation Française' and get my student book signed by a professor in order to draw my miserable stipend of 15 dollars a month. This sinister shadow would sneak after me even through the echoing marble halls of the Sorbonne until I ducked into the full flood of chattering French students in which I would lose him or think I had. No such luck. There he would be hanging in some dark doorway or hiding behind a lamp post to skid out and slither after me until he had me practically running all the way home. I told our housekeeper Fiona about this and she offered to beat him up for me. She was that big and tough, she could have.

'I know the one you mean,' she laughed. 'Tall, dark and thin as a rake, isn't he? Well under thirty but sort of stooped over, no? He's a Greek who lives in that little fleabag hotel without a name up our alley. He's been trying to get Antonia to invite him for ages. We all call him Mr Grease.'

He cornered me, finally, in Sylvia Beach's bookshop, Shakespeare and Co. There was nothing Sylvia could do but introduce us. He forced her hand. He was good at it. The Greeks know no shame. I turned to leave but he followed me out, inviting me for a drink on the terrace of a nearby café. When the time came to pay, he said he had no money. He had ordered himself an expensive whisky and a pack of imported cigarettes. I had to pay for them, too. Back in Athens, he claimed, his family was rich, very rich, but because of some trouble he had with the new regime down there, trouble over some political poems he had published, he was an exile in Paris. Owing to the bothersome currency restriction imposed by his enemies, no one could send him any money from Greece. His mother would if she could but his father was furious with him. When he suggested we dine in a Greek restaurant in the Latin Quarter where he would introduce me to Greek food and retsina wine, I guessed I would have to pay for that too. I said, thanks very much but no thanks. I was wising up. Where did I dine? It wasn't quite true but I said I always dined with my cousin Antonia. I was not about to invite him into the house even when he followed me right up to the door. To get shut of him, I practically slammed the heavy door in his face but at once he began knocking loudly. When I poked my head out, he said he was hungry. I slipped him 5 francs in a fury.

On Antonia's very next Day, there he was in the house, having attached himself to Sylvia and her real heavy French girlfriend Adrienne to invite himself in along with them. Birdlike Sylvia Beach was in charge of those English language writers in Paris like James Joyce and Hemingway, while lumbering Adrienne Monnier, who had a French language bookshop across the same street, was in charge of the French writers of note like Gide and Cocteau. Those were two more you really had to watch out for. And creepy little old Marcel Jouhandeau – oh Wow! Wandering hands. But the Greek had them beat. Within the week, there he was all the time up in my private quarters on the top floor, eating and drinking every night along with me and my few young friends. They all hated him on sight. I guess I got drunk. The next thing I knew, he had gotten so drunk he passed out on my bed where I found him snoring next morning when I woke up on the floor. Remember the story about the Arab who let his camel put just its nose under the edge of his tent? He woke up next morning to find himself out in the Sahara while his camel snored on beside him, comfortably wrapped up in his canvas. I simply could not get rid of this man. When they finally threw him out of his nameless hotel up our side street, he moved in on me permanently. And Antonia never even knew. He was wise enough to keep out of her way. The house was big enough. He intercepted my mail, read my letters, poked into my private papers, tried to worm every last Family secret out of me, psychoanalysed every last thing I said or did. He never let up on me. Sometimes he amused me. He knew or had known practically everybody and he was as full of maliciously spicy gossip as any good Greek. I was all ears, of course. He went out of his way to titillate me with tall tales about all the great ladies who gathered in Antonia's house on her Days and especially about those who stayed on for her secret sessions in Joan of Arc's chapel. We could hear them stomping around raising raucous hell down there under us.

'You know,' mused my Greek, 'I do believe your bathroom in there is directly above the high altar. Don't you just long to get a peek at what they're up to down there? I'll bet we could. If we could crawl in under that false floor of your bathroom where the plumbers get in, maybe we could drill a hole through the ceiling and look down on them directly. I dare you.'

We could and we did. It was all pretty crazy. I don't really like to look back on it even now, all these years later. I was disgusted and scared. But there was an outrageously funny side to it, too, that made me want to laugh hysterically when I first caught sight of the mad mêlée going on down there below in the chapel. A lot of those lovely ladies on the far side of their menopause were horsing around with their girlfriends dressed up as cowboys, shrieking, '*Hi-Ho Silver!*' at the top of their lungs, while an old Roy Rogers record was bawling out 'Home on the Range'. Clad in studded leather chaps with ten-gallon hats clapped on their fair heads, they were stomping around in their cowboy boots, jumping on each other's backs playing horsey. A couple of couples would run full tilt at each other until all four of these gay old girls were rolling around on the floor splitting their britches with laughter. Then Cousin Antonia appeared and what seemed to have begun as a wild game became something much more serious, more deadly. She waved her arms about and threw back her head to let out an earpiercing yodel. It didn't sound the least like her. All her adepts fell into a chorus line, baying like banshees or bloodhounds giving voice after their quarry, a man, Orpheus the Poet who had spied on their mysteries. My blood ran cold and turned into water. A bonedeep chill ran all through me because, in those days, I thought of myself as a poet.

Stifling in the tight spot we had wedged ourselves into, I thought it was all part of the nightmare when I felt the hot breath of this Greek in my ear as he hissed, 'I'm going to tell your cousin Antonia we did this unless you do what I say, let me do what I want to you, right here and now, do you hear me?'

He was fumbling with the buttons on the fly of my English tailored trousers and I had to admit that my young cock was as hard as a rod, excited into a state of almost painful erection by the weirdly erotic scene down below. The ladies were letting down more than their hair as he poked his penis between my bare feet while he sucked me off avidly, deepthroating me. It was the first time anyone ever did this to me and I really didn't dig it that much. It sort of disgusted me. But what was a poor boy to do?

What I did was to look around the house for a girl or woman. There was one fairly young hanger-on around the house whom I found slightly seductive, the more I thought about it. She was a dark White Russian ex-princess named Natasha, naturally, who seemed unattached. I learned later that she was fairly recently divorced from a Rumanian diplomat who had caught her *in flagrante delicto* with a girlfriend. Down one of the mysterious dark corridors of the vast house hung with tapestries, I waylaid her. Pulling the dusty old arras around us, I grabbed her and kissed her. To my surprise, she went off like a fire alarm, smearing her red lipstick all over my face, shocking me into an instant erection as I fought for my breath with her tongue in my tonsils. At the same time, she would not let me lay hands on her sex but caught my hot mitts with her claws to press them against her big breasts, instructing my fingers how to roll her nipples between them, 'making bread' like a blind kitten does to its mother. She pants and she moans, twisting her knees together like a little girl who wants to make pipi, squeezing her thighs until she begins to come like a rainbow, biting into my milky young neck while running her fingernails up and down the nobs on my spine until I tingle all over like a tomcat. But I still don't have my cock out. As soon as it's over for her, she goes for my face with her nails, snarling like a tiger or tigress, I guess I should say. Flinging me off her, she slaps my face twice with a forehand and a backhand and goes storming away down the dark passage without looking back once, furiously combing the sparks out of her long black hair.

'What the hell was all that about?' I asked my Greek when he discovered her marks on me. 'Didn't she like me or what?'

'That standup whore!' he raged, mad with jealousy, 'her Rumanian husband divorced her because she would never let him get into her. She would never let him penetrate her with his penis. She must have a very tough hymen because she's been selling her virginity to a lot of rich old lesbian ladies like your cousin Antonia who gave her the famous *Coup du Colonel* and it didn't even work on her.'

'The *Coup du Colonel*, what's that?' I asked eagerly.

My Greek was always full of lurid details about the revolting things he preached to me under the banners of Freud and Marx and Trotsky. At that tender age, I was transfixed and goggle-eyed. He was forever planning and plotting and preaching and poetizing, too, in the coupled names of snotty young Rimbaud, that was me, and his rotten old lover Verlaine. The Greek hung around my young life like the Old Man of the Sea, taking on different slimy shapes and sizes at any old hour of the day or night. He still had no money but he kept on inviting me to stay in his parents' palace in Athens that summer. All I had to do was to get enough money out of Antonia for us to sail off together to Greece. In Greece, he would pay me back double so I could send one half back to pay off Antonia and live off the rest all that summer. Getting money, cash money out of Antonia was not all that easy. No matter how little you asked for, she would give you a little less than half that amount, pleading poverty. I know just how she felt when you ask me for money. We left for Greece in extremely reduced circumstances as deck passengers on a boat from Marseilles.

Before we took off, I had my first woman, thanks to him too. He introduced her as a childhood friend from nursery days in Athens when they had played house together. They played doctor and nurse a bit later. Then they played postman at parties and petted. By the age of thirteen, she was his girl. She was hot stuff. Even before she grew tits, he said with a leer, she had 'quite a reputation'. When she showed up in Paris, he brought her around to one of Antonia's Days. On sight, Antonia hated her. Heleni Argolaki was the Greek shipping heiress aged twenty-one, just exactly two years and six months and two days older than I was. In Real Time, perhaps, she had at least a couple of centuries on me. Although she was married, the newspapers still called her The Richest Little Girl in the World.

'Why,' she laughed, when we met under the frosty gaze of

Cousin Antonia and her assembled Ladies, 'we were *made* for each other! We must celebrate this at once if not sooner. My husband would just love this but fortunately he's gone back to Athens with his nurse and the baby.'

'Love me, *Agapemou!*' was the first Greek word she taught me in the taxi as she very nearly slammed the car door on the hand of Mr Grease, our Greek, our mutual Greek who was trying to scramble in after me. 'Hotel Regina!' she snapped to the driver. Whatever she said was like that, an order.

When we got out of the taxi in front of the gilded equestrian statue of Joan of Arc in full armour, she said, 'That's why I love the Hotel Regina.' I was still wondering what she might mean by that as she propelled me through the revolving doors of this staid old hotel in the shadow of the Louvre. So, that's why she didn't stay at the Ritz like anyone civilized. The uniformed flunkeys within bowed low and no wonder. She looked like the *Vogue* magazine picture of several too many millions of dollars on stiletto heels. Topped by a towering surrealist hat like a lobster pot with a live lobster in it and tricked out by Schiaparelli, she was painted and varnished like a Byzantine ikon reeking of something called Shocking. It gave me an asthma attack, *instanter*. I very nearly collapsed in the hotel elevator. The sniggering bellboy seemed to think I was panting after her and maybe she did too from the look on her. I was practically down on all fours as I followed her down along the upholstered halls of the hotel to her seemingly endless suite of rooms.

'That's your bathroom in there,' she advised me. 'There's a blue dressing-gown hanging up there. I'm going to slip into something more comfortable. You'll find me in here.'

When I did find her in there, I didn't recognize her. She may not have recognized me either, as I stood there with nothing on but my stinky argyll socks and my only slightly soiled boxer shorts, gawking at her and breathing with difficulty. We stood there for a long endless look, like strangers. Out from under that aggressive hat and down off those threatening stiletto heels, her face wiped clear of her theatrical make-up, she had lost the shell of sophistication it all gave her. Down on her own bare brown feet, with her shiny black hair falling down over her bare breasts with dark nipples, she looked like some little Greek peasant girl from the islands being offered for sale to the Turks. Or maybe, just maybe, antique Andromeda chained to her rock. When she jumped head-first into the huge French double bed, she flashed me the full moon of the first woman's bare ass I had ever seen. I noticed the soles of her feet were dirty. My asthma suddenly let go of my lungs as it can at times, abruptly. With a wild war-whoop, I jumped after her into the hay.

I performed quite well, I think, several times in a row before she began to show me a few new ways, new ways to me at least, new ways to do it. As time went on, what began to worry me was the extent of her own satisfaction. Was she enjoying this, really? Maybe I wasn't doing so good since the first few times around she was mum, with never a word or a moan out of her. Was this all right? I tried harder. Each assault was taking more out of me and took longer until, finally, she began to murmur and then to say and then to yell and then to scream, 'No! No! NOOOOOOOOOOO!' What the hell was the matter, didn't she like it? Or what? Women began by being a mystery to me and throughout a long life have remained so. So much the better. I understand I am not alone in this. It doesn't really worry me all that much but sometimes I do wonder. What *did* I do wrong? Then or ever?

The next time I saw her was a couple of months later that hellishly hot summer in Athens, in the bar of the Megali Brittania, the old Grande Bretagne Hotel. She was dressed all in black, chic Paris black, painted like an idol and covered with jewels, sitting small in a huge tapestried chair like a throne, surrounded by a pack of fawning Greek courtiers, not another woman in sight. For her and for me, there was no one else in sight but us two, I think, as I strode across the shining marble floor to her. I just said hello but did not take her hand or bend over to kiss her. She looked up brightly and said, 'Go get your gear together and be back here in an hour. My captain has just phoned from Piraeus to say we must sail before sunset.' All the surrounding Greeks held their breath, you could hear it. You could hear things clicking together in their ivory skulls like a break in a pool game. All their ideas about Heleni and her millions were adjusting themselves almost audibly. Not one more word need be said. They knew all about us. Yes, just from her words and her tone of voice, they knew all about us or they thought they did. They did not know about me, though, except what they read in the newspapers. If there was one more word to be said, it would have to be said by me, so I said it.

'No,' I said. 'No, I can't. I am sorry.'

And I was terribly, desperately, sickeningly sorry. I had just come from the doctor who told me my Wasserman blood test was positive, I had syphilis. In those long-ago days, penicillin was still a whole World War Two away ahead of us. Syphilis was then a matter for suicide. Years, many years of painful treatment were not sure to wipe the last trace of it out of your bloodstream or save you from a long long lingering death-in-life. The worst! The Bible says you can pass it on to your children *even unto the third and fourth generation*!

Poor Helenaki, she thought she had a bad enough secret for me but I had an even worse one for her.

Her husband was divorcing her because she was pregnant. Apparently, he had every reason to believe this child was not his. She said it was mine. How could she know, really *know* this? How could *I* know? I had every reason not to want to believe her. I started counting on my fingers. Incubation means counting. How long does it take for syphilis to incubate? How long does it take for a baby? Count the days, count the weeks, count the months, count the moons and the suns and the nights that led up to this. How long does it take to forget a story like this? I hope to have forgotten it before I wake up in the morning.

What day is this, Adam? How long, oh how long have I been in the Bardo? Life was just one long sequence of questions: is death going to be, too? I wonder.

'Don't you have any health insurance, Blue Cross, Medicare, Social Security, anything like that?' Dr Adam is expostulating all over me. 'There *is* the matter of my fee, you know!'

'You've got to be joking,' I mumble. 'At this late date? I couldn't afford it. I haven't got any money, cash money, never did. Everything's all tied up in securities, properties, my Museum. Can't touch it. Nobody can.'

'All you rich kids, you super-rich kids, give me a swift pain in the prostate. You're all the same, every last one of you. Ask you for money and what do you get? Excuses. The best one can hope for is a bum cheque, a little bouncy cheque, a sheaf of chic autumn leaves. I happen to know you never paid your old school tailor. And me?' Adam splutters all over me, 'And me? You know how much I always got for an hour of analytical therapy? You know how much it costs to run a place like the Bardo?'

'Not much. It shouldn't cost much. Accommodation as shabby as this should cost nothing. The Tibetans or whoever it is ought to pay us to stay here. Instead of which, we all have to pay the earth to get into this dump, the whole earth! The whole earth and everything in it. Where does all that wealth go? To Tibet? Do the Tibetans issue our Visas, our Exit and Entry Permits, collect the rent? There's something wrong here, something very wrong. After all, I own this place. It's all mine, in my name. I own the Bardo Hotel, I invented it. These Tibetans are my tenants, after all. They bore me, bore me to death, quite literally. I don't trust them, never did. I put the Egyptians on the front door, the street door, to keep a close tab on their comings and their goings. Cheats and liars, all religions ought to be taxed out of existence. It was understood in our contract that they were to keep Madame Ra on forever.'

'You mean Madame Rachou, don't you?'

'I know what I mean. I feel I'm being swindled. Things are not going as I had planned them anywhere. I can't quite see how all this is going to end. Can you?'

'Well, sort of. I've taken a degree in that too, in Necromancy, as a mattra fack, came from the same or, more correctly, through the same mail order source in California as my others. All equally valuable. Everything, anything, that's what we're here for. I'm your doctor, only your doctor, not your fortune-teller, and that's what you're asking. How can I tell when or where it is all going to end? I'm not writing this, you are. I'm here only because you are.'

'What I want is something like a statistical study I can understand.'

'Too late, too late! Madame Ra Chou has taken her account book with her, her hotel register and all the identity papers deposited with her before they flew her to Palmdale or Los Angeles airport or wherever. Nowadays, Madame Ra sets in the West as Ra does, in the West where the Sun dies every night in the Pacific. You should know all that, you're a Westerner, yourself, aren't you?'

'As I was saying before I was so rudely interrupted, I'm an American and I want to see some facts and figures.'

'Big Nurse doesn't release her figures. She sticks to the rules. A Room a Day. A Floor a Week. Forty-nine Rooms in the Hotel. Rooms must be vacated daily. You see the privileges you get with your money, even here. What's left of the Hotel Bardo is revolving around you.'

'And as it should, as it ought, as it must, it has to. This is MY hotel. As you say, I am writing it or, rather, I am writing it if you say so. Me, I don't buy that for one second, one single second. Why would I write myself into a situation this miserable?'

'Complain complain complain! Oh, dearie me, what a kuf-*fuffle*! You have only your self to blame and you know it. Apart from the privileges showered, positively showered over you, my dear, everything is going on schedule.'

'But those upper floors up there, is it worth it? What goes on up there? When you do make it up there, is it worth it? Why am I being kept in the dark down here on the Fourth Floor of my own hotel and no one can tell me exactly what's going on upstairs? Surely Mickey must know, and Violet.'

'Neither one of them's talking, not even in AMSLAN.'

'When I first took on the place, they told tales of a blithe spirit singing away up there on the very top floor, in the attics, singing up there like a lark, a lark with a little lead in its wings but a lark all the same, Gregorio Corsorio. He had a whole chorus of blonde Scandinavian girls with crowns of burning candles on their heads who lined the spiral spinal staircase in perpetual adoration singing an endless chorus like a litany, 'Grrregggooooorio! Gregggorrrriyoooo Corsaorrrriyooooo!' I thought that so charming that I bought the place sight unseen and unheard, on mere hearsay. You may say I behaved stupidly, quixotically, oxitacally, outrageously, I don't care, really. I am that I am, and that's all there is to it.'

'If there's one thing I hate it's birds. Pigeons, larks, anything with hot dusty dry feathers, vermin of the air, shitting all over the place, ugh! As for the birdsong you're talking about, Mickey blew out the sound system long ago, playing his own *Greatest Hits* so loud he burnt his huge amps and couldn't replace them, not here. Before that happy day, people were always complaining to Madame Rachou about the awful noise but she had a soft spot for him like she did for all young ones who had been in jail. Big Nurse isn't like that at all.'

'I thought you said you couldn't jail a monkey. When was Mickey Monkey in jail?'

'Not Mickey, Gregorio grew up in jail, so he claims. That's what made him such a good poet. All poets ought to be jailed.'

'I don't want to take up any more of your time, doctor. I've always thought of myself as a poet.'

'Before I go, there's this matter of my fee . . .' he begins again.

'Fuck you and your fee!' I explode. 'I want out of here. Give me a shot, a hotshot of something. I'm wasting my time here with you. I wanna go, you hear?'

'Go? Go where? Upstairs? I want to go too. I'm only here because you are.'

'You seem to be something more than my doctor, Adam, are you my friend?'

'I am not your friend and never really was.'

'Well, that's frank of you. This conversation could be getting dangerous, couldn't it?'

'It sure could but I'm not hiding anything from you about your condition, your condition and mine, I might add. Even I don't know exactly how you get out of here or up there or whatever. I don't know. Both Violet and Mickey have led me to believe that it's easier for them, you know, animals and the lower orders, simple people with simple ideas, true believers and all them.'

'I see. That is, I don't see. You tell me there is a staircase out there, a spiritual, no, I mean a spiral, a spyratual staircase right under my window. Who's that out there right now? It sounds like a lot of Moroccan women on market day and someone is smoking some great grass.'

'I thought you couldn't smell.'

'I lived in Morocco long enough to learn how to smell through my ears and see through my nose. That's the best thing I've smelt since I lost my breath.'

'That's a gang of women waiting for Shereefa to appear in the doorway of her shrine. Her shrine is in Room Twenty-four, second next to you. She's going to do a Transfiguration or a Transmogrification or something, she told me, give the girls their money's worth, she said. That'll be the day.'

'Is that Jane's Shereefa who sold wheat from her stall in the market under the palm trees next to the Commissariat of Police in Tangier? It can't be.'

'It is. When she got back from Antonia's Annual Party, she moved up here and set up her shrine.'

'From Antonia's? I can't believe that. I don't remember Antonia having any Moroccans in her coterie nor even in her kitchen.'

'Shereefa was there at the very last Annual Party. She knows *all* the Gurls. She knows everybody, all the Gurls everywhere. You just can't imagine how important she's become. She's got even the Tibetans under her thumb. She picked up on the lingo and all that from their women.'

'The lingo but not the lingam, I suspect.'

'The lingam? What's that? Oh, I know what you mean. No, Shereefa's into the *muni*, exclusively.'

'Pretty deep into it, too, I'll bet.'

'Oh yes, she's got a 21-centimetre clitoris. She'll be stopping in here before she goes out to expose herself to her faithful on the stairs.'

'Expose herself? Great God, no! Don't let her in here. I don't want to have to see that. I remember poor naked Janie, one cold winter day just before they locked her up for good, asking me if I wanted to see her pussy. I didn't. I don't.'

'You don't have to. You can't.'

'Oh, can't I! I told you I can see with my nose.'

'I'm afraid there's going to be a riot out there. The noble young man I was telling you about, who has the duplex across the stairwell with his tiny terrorist tramp, has invited in a whole restaurantful of these Thai transvestites he's been having creepy sex with, the whole reptile house. I don't think Shereefa's followers are going to like that one bit. They'll think somebody is making fun of them, dressing up like that, dressing up as women.'

'Why? I would have thought they'd be flattered by people dressing up as women who don't have to. Personally, I always found transvestites revolting. I don't know why, when I come to think of it, but I don't want to go into that, either. And this is the young man you want me to meet. Why?'

'He wants to meet you, insists on it. Says he's got something to tell you. Something important, important to you.'

'OK, doc, just let me sleep on it.'

So, here I am back in my Greece again where I swore the wild horses of my father Neptune could never drag me. I'll never get cured of this place. It's in my blood still, perhaps because I so nearly became immortal there that hot summer before I was twenty. On the island of Naxos with vine leaves in my hair, I just missed becoming the young god, Dionysus. Everything pointed to it. I had fever and chills and terrible headaches, a sore throat. The rigging of the ship on which I sailed through the unstilled Cyclades suddenly budded and broke out green leaves, ivy and laurel grew into wreaths around the lifebuoys. The Greek sailors chanted and danced on the deck like inebriates before throwing themselves into the wine-dark sea to become the sporting dolphins who piloted us into port. And on that island of Naxos I met Ariadne, as mythology had it. She was a girl from Crete who had been abandoned there by an Athenian politician in exile named Theseus.

Poor pregnant Helenaki rolled up the window between us and the chauffeur of her immense old Hitlerian Mercedes so we could have a heart to heart talk as we drove down to Piraeus where her yacht lay. The late summer sun was setting blood-red below a towering purple storm blowing up over Athens from the Aegean. Boiling black clouds overhead were being ripped to shreds by Poseidon's forked lightning directed against the shining Acropolis. With her sharp stony profile set against the rain washing the car window, she said, 'We are not friends, are we? I barely know you.' It was sickening to have to tell her any part of my own sordid story but she seemed not to be listening to what little I told her. Her chauffeur, catching my eye in his rearview mirror, winked at me as if he heard what was said, or was he flirting with me? I was horrified by his effrontery but that's the Greeks for you. I shut up but it was my turn to be turned into stone when she told me her story.

'As you can see, I am in mourning,' she said, 'first of all for my father and mother but more recently for my baby. In a high sea off Crete last week, his nurse lost him overboard and jumped after him before anyone knew it on board. I had to come back to Athens on business and to meet you, apparently, but now I am on my way back to join the search party. I am afraid we will find nothing in these shark-infested waters. He has suffered a seachange. These are the pearls that were his eyes. These are the tiny pink shells that were his hands.'

There was nothing to say to that, was there?

'His name was Spiro Dionysus and that is the name of my yacht. My ship's chandlers have made us a set of black sails overnight, like the ones they made for Theseus. We Greeks are still living in mythological time. That's how I can bear it. This child of ours,' she said, running her jewelled hands over her belly, 'if he has this disease of yours, may turn out to be a real mythological monster. What do you think, would you like that?'

Her diamonds were winking viciously as she brushed a sparkling tear from her eye. My throat was thick and painful. I had chancres inside both corners of my mouth. I was contagious. I could not kiss her.

Aboard the *Dionysus* there was champagne on deck and there was our ineffable water rat, Mr Grease, flirting outrageously with the sailors. I stumbled on board blind with fury at the idea we both had to go to his doctor, his 'skin specialist', as they were called politely. I grabbed the champagne to get drunk as quick as I could, nursing the idea of hitting him over the head with the bottle and dropping him into the harbour. The buffet table, set out with paper-thin cucumber sandwiches, was decorated with vine leaves which he wove into a fillet and passed to Heleni to crown me Dionysus. Snarling, I tore it off my head and threw it into the filthy garbage floating on the oily port waters as I staggered towards the gangplank which was narrow. I caught a glimpse of her bosun, Heleni's boatswain, as he ran his lascivious hot black Greek eyes over my too tight white summer pants, brazenly. When he licked his greasy lips, I charged at him like a ram. A sailor caught me, respectfully, as though to help me, but he helped me far too insistently, I thought, letting his horny hand slide far too far down the small of my back. Like the young Dionysus in those far-off days, my forms were fluent and remarkably rounded. None of these grinning Gricks needed *Dent's Smaller Classical Dictionary*, London 1910, to read: *'The form of his body is manly but approaches the female form by its softness and roundness. In works of art he appears as a youthful god. His expression is languid and his attitude is easy like that of a man who is absorbed in sweet thought or is slightly intoxicated.'* Only the last word applied. I was so drunk I very nearly fell into the harbour. *'Youthful, beautiful but effeminate god of wine'*, indeed! I wanted to kill myself.

I ran pellmell down the quai, cutting blindly through the throngs of hysterical Greeks loaded with luggage, pushing and pulling and screaming as if they had just escaped from the Turkish massacres in Asia Minor. My own Greek came running after me, screaming.

When he caught me, we fought. I flailed at him blindly but he wouldn't fight back, letting men in the crowd pull me off him. 'I'm not going one more step with you anywhere ever!' I cried. 'Not even to the doctor's. I can't stand any more of those hotshots of Salvarsan in my veins and the cheeks of my ass are sore, swollen hard as a board with bismuth. I'm going away somewhere. I need a holiday. A long holiday from you, you shit.'

In a nearby low-down café heavy with the odour of hashish, he gave me some of the money he owed me, owed me and Antonia, and he wrote me the name Thamyra in Greek. This was a blind peasant poetess who lived in the mountains on the island of Naxos. She had been in Athens that previous winter giving recitals of her poetry to elegant audiences in Athenian salons. She was well-known on her island. All I had to do was to ask for her. With no luggage at all, he put me on the night boat leaving for the unstilled Cyclades. I would have a rough passage, outside the harbour the Meltemi was blowing. As I went aboard, he pointed out that this ship called the *Theseus* belonged to the Argolaki Line. I had to stop him from telling the ship's purser on board that I was a friend of the family and therefore had nothing to pay.

The little inter-island steamer was as filthy as all Greek ships are, its open decks packed with peasants in black who seemed to be going to a mass funeral somewhere. Someone told me they were pilgrims bound for the holy island of Tinos where they have a miraculous Virgin. There were tight family groups around children bawling for food. Great golden loaves were broken and passed from hand to hand to be eaten with dead-white goat cheese and wrinkled black olives to be washed down with retsina, their bitter white wine. A few fathers became tipsy and violent quarrels broke out and were as suddenly subsided. Those who had secured the best places defended them against all comers as they huddled close to the steam pipes or sought a winkbreak before we got out into the open sea.

Just then a rusty old woman in black hobbled down the quay screaming as she dragged a great big shaggy copper-coated goat behind her. Moaning that she was a poor old woman and nobody ever waited for her, she drove the tawny beast up the gangplank just as it lifted and threw them both flat on the deck at my feet. The goat jerked free of her, bucked and clattered out a warning tattoo with his cloven hooves as he got his bearings. I stood between him and the companionway. He cocked his bronze horns and shot me a chilling glance of recognition out of one malevolent golden eye. I feinted as he flashed by me with one flying leap down into the thick of the deck passengers below.

Pandemonium, literally, broke out down there. Brave men grabbed at the big ram, but he worked like a boxer with horns and they fell back in comic surprise, trampling those behind them. Whole families set to drubbing each other with baskets and bundles exploding while children sat wailing, smeared with food. The orange goat bounded everywhere. He was a whole flock of goats and he swept the deck. Only a mother and child were left stranded under the cold searchlights which suddenly came on, turning it into theatre. The sight of these actors made me sag over the rail with a lurch of sick curiosity. This drab woman the colour of ancient dust was being yanked and dragged around by her husky little boy as he lunged after the goat, roaring and bellowing. Mother and child were coupled by a yard or more of chain riveted around her waist and his. She could just restrain him but it was a real struggle. He might have been eight or ten and big for his age but still a child. He was a child except for his huge, his monstrous head. His lowering great head was set on a powerfully arched neck, silky with tight black hair that grew down like a pelt over his naked shoulders. He bellowed until foam flew from his muzzle. He had the head of a young bull. His mother, a peasant Pasiphae, strained at the tether that bound her to her baby Minotaur.

The heat in my cabin was intolerable. As soon as our ship shuddered under weigh, I plunged into nightmares. I was shut in a coffin with a slamming lid. One golden eye with a vertical pupil swam through the crack an inch from my own eye. The goat! I dragged my body back to life with a superhuman effort like Lazarus. My cabin door was slamming back and forth with the pitch of our ship. I staggered to my feet, my head pounding with fever, to hear the clatter of the goat's hooves out on deck – or was it the engines? I couldn't breathe. Air, I must have air!

Piled up even in front of my door, the pilgrims slept wrapped up in their sheets like mummies. Under the harsh decklights, it looked like a scene in a plague hospital. Ah, the great disaster, I thought resignedly, they were trying to escape the eruption and now they have all been overtaken and are dead. The damp night air was a palpable blanket, a shroud through which one could hardly breathe. I fumbled around until I found the brass catch to my cabin door and fell back into dark cthonic underground mythological dreams.

The clanking of a donkey-engine woke me about midnight when I looked out to see we had put into the brilliantly lit little port of Syra. The sleepers had vanished. We were drawn up close alongside the quay like a stage boat run in on the set for an operetta. I could almost reach out to touch the flat walls of houses painted rosy coral and pale lemon-yellow under pink tiled roofs. I dropped a coin to the scuttling waiter below on the terrace of a busy restaurant full of elegant summer people in starched white who ate seafood at tables set out on the cobbled quay right under our bow. The lame lurching wail of a Greek tango ran on like a forgotten tap. The town clock in a tower hammered out midnight on its cracked bell. Before the waiter could bring me a bowl of iced Corinthian seedless grapes, a choir of massed voices swelled down a narrow street from which the pilgrims wound out waving green branches and carrying garlands of ivy. They swept blindly through the diners and up the gangplank on to our ship. The waiter stood to attention with my grapes and crossed himself with a napkin.

The pilgrims chanted lustily as they hung our ship with green. Our masts stood like stripped trees whose branches lay piled about their feet. Vines coiled like cordage: ivy twined through the rigging. Our lifebuoys became laurel wreaths. Our whole ship burgeoned into a floating island bursting with leaves. Our sailors took up the chant and leaped about wildly, casting off green ropes. Our next port was the holy island of Tinos to which the poor pilgrims were bound. Tinos is rock-barren: they had gathered this verdure to freshen her shrine. I slept through their debarkation, still deep in the green smell of broken branches, to wake only with sunstruck Naxos straight ahead. There was not a single sailor on deck but a school of friendly dolphins sporting in our glassy furrow piloted us into port. Leaning far over the prow, I was more than tempted to throw myself overboard after them but at that sacred moment a quite good-looking Greek cabin steward came up behind me to put his hot hand on my ass, my sore ass! I hauled off and hit him one.

I thought afterwards that a contagious kiss from me would have been much more like divine punishment from a sick young demigod on the run for his life, his more than life, his immortality.

Doors are slamming and slamming all over the Bardo. People

are leaving and more people are coming up the stairs. All hell is breaking loose out there. When and where have I heard this noise before? Adam just burst into my room again blubbering, completely hysterical as only an old anti-psychiatrist can be. There was so much noise, so much screaming and yelling of oriental ladies tearing their veils off and tearing the lining out of their throats that I could not hear a word he was saying.

'Shut up!' I snapped. 'I could kill you! You know what you've just done to me, don't you? You've just yanked me back here into restraint, back from the best time of my life when I very nearly became the god Dionysus. I was beginning, just beginning to sense the godhead coming down on me like a mantle, like an incandescent helmet as hot as a hairdrier when you barged in here. What the hell is all that row going on out there?'

'It's magnificent, as you say, mythological! It's the battle between the Amazons and the Harpies. Shereefa's hamfisted heavy Moroccan ladies are beating the shit out of Yaya's fairy crew of Thailandese transvestites.'

'Who? What?'

'It's the Hags versus the Fags, colossal spectacle! A magnificent pitched battle on the stairs out there. All the more exciting because of the multiple confusions of the sexes. Young Yaya de la Foutaise started all this. His fat-assed little terrorist tramp he calls his "Camarade" became wildly jealous of the way he was carrying on with this whole tong gang of cold-blooded oriental reptiles in drag. They have opened a string of not all that cheap chop suey parlours all up and down our old street, completely ruining its original cachet. Being Buddhists, they have an'in'with the Tibetans, naturally or unnaturally. Foutaise prefers them the latter way and has them both in and out, up and in, if you follow me.'

'I don't intend to.'

'Freaky or whatever he calls his freeloading so-called "room-mate" claims she can't sleep a wink, nor with a Tiddly-wink either, so she flips out and lands on them on the landing. At which point . . .'

'Hey, wait a minute, wait another minute! Who *are* these people? Am I supposed to know them? De la Foutaise does sound vaguely familiar. I think I once knew a beautiful boy of that name but I can't remember where or when, long ago at my boarding school, maybe. He had a first name like a girl's, I seem to recall, but you call him Yaya. With all this mixup in names, I guess ya gotta get the printed programme to tell what sexes these people are in, doncha.'

'Not even a racing form won't help all that much, the way the dark horses are running around here. I don't know myself any more. Young Yaya de la Foutaise has been fooling around sexually with this whole subculture of cunning little oriental drag queens who work as waitresses in these chop suey par-lours, Viets Thais Laotians Cambodians you name it, they're all Chinks, Tiddlywinks. They've become known as the Rice Bowl and any fool who falls in with them is called a Rice Queen. It's also known as the Yellow Disease and it's spread through the West because of those boat people out there. Once you've caught it, your old lovers will know you no more. Foutaise had earlier attacks of Jungle Fever but a chocolate-coloured Jungle Bunny known as Baby Blackjack, a promising monicker, turned out to be more of a lady than the Laotian ladies who can throw an armlock on you, flip you over and fuck you up the ass before you can say Tiddlywinks. Yaya sur-rounds himself with these saurians. Nothing normal or healthy about him, he prefers creepy kicks. Almost too much for me and I'm a medical man. I've had sex sessions with him, as I told you. I think he's a bit of a gerontophile. Even you might score there, old man. He's got a 21-centimetre penis, I measured it.'

'You make me sick with your sex talk. All that's over for me years ago. Since I was so thoroughly butchered on the operat-ing table, I can neither fuck nor be fucked. I can come, only just, but I can't get it up hard any more. Anybody would have to be crazy to want to go to bed with me. I'll never have sex again, never.'

'Never say never, above all in the Bardo. Besides, Foutaise *is* crazy. He was crazy enough to go and lose his hands in that last accident of his career as a terrorist. However, *he* never says die. He is firmly convinced he'll get them back intact on the next floor up. He had fine hands and was ordinately proud of them. A pity, but that's the sort of thing always happens.'

'How did he lose them?'

'In the explosion. Manipulating a hand grenade at a summer school for rich upper-class terrorist children run by Trotskyites in Brittany. As you said, just the sort of place where they teach them how to shoot their uncles in the knees. They converted him while he was in his first year at Sciences Politiques. They made a Marxist marquis out of him. That's one story. The other is that it happened while he was sticking plastic explosive to the base of Antoine Dolet's statue in the Place Maubert. That's what he told his right-wing family. Both tales may well be apocryphal since he isn't talking. He's a born conspirator, knows how to keep his mouth shut.'

'More than I ever knew how to do. I remember there was Marxist propaganda being spread at my British boarding school even in my day. Beats me. Look at that bunch of upper-class traitors from Eton and Oxford. Burgess and Philby and MacLean and them. Ended up being cremated and entombed in the wall of the Kremlin. No comment.'

'Yes, he's a sly one. Oh by the way, before I forget: Shereefa's coming to see you, have a talk.'

'Oh, no she's not. I've got nothing to say to Shereefa. Besides, my meagre kitchen and bedroom Moroccan Arabic deserted me long ago. Like my Greek, I never learned to read and write in those languages and you have to, you know, to really digest them.'

'Digest them? You talk about language like as if it was something to eat and drink.'

'Isn't it? Don't we say things like "hungry for praise", or "thirsting after it"? "I drank in your words", or "I'll make you eat your own words". How about that? Don't we? Without words, we wouldn't exist.'

'We don't, old boy. We don't exist any more, at least not

officially but we're still using language, aren't we?'

'What's that you say? With all that hullabaloo out there, I can't hear you. What were you saying about Shereefa?'

'Shereefa's become very important here in the Bardo. She could help you.'

'God forbid! Protect me from being helped, as you call it, by her. When she moves in on you, Shereefa helps herself to everything you've got including your sanity. She's the evil native witch in a short story by Conrad or Maugham or Bowles. She's the sinister servant you can't get rid of before she gets rid of you. She poisons the parrot or your pet Pekinese just to show you she holds the power of life and death over you and you can't escape until you've handed over to her whatever it is she wants from you. Poor Jane! Everyone in Tangier knew that Shereefa . . .'

At this point I hear old Adam burbling, 'This is an honour, Your Holiness. Here is the Shereefa in your doorway, right now. Come in, Your Holiness.'

Caught in a tight corner like that, there is only one thing to do and I did it. Knock yourself out: become unconscious. So, I pretended to fall asleep as old crocks like me often do, suddenly. I must have put on a good show for them because there they were, Adam and Shereefa as thick as thieves in a thicket, discussing the whole Bardo booking procedure over my body as if I were dead. They tell us that when we are dead or just about dead, the last sense to leave us is hearing. Chances are, the last words you hear said are the doctor's saying: The patient is dead. I could hear every word they were saying, of course. They were both lying their heads off, trying to impress each other. I was amazed. Here she was claiming she picked up the *Coup du Colonel* from my Cousin Antonia, when I knew for a fact that Antonia never crossed the colour line in her lifetime. Maybe afterwards. To make it all more revolting, there was old Adam calling Shereefa Your Holiness. It was Your Holiness this and Your Holiness that and even 'Her Holiness is absolutely right.' Imagine.

Her Holiness, indeed! I can remember her when. Jane was

the one who took us all down to her little arched stone stall to smoke grass and eat soup during Ramadan. Her stall from which she sold measures of wheat was one in a row of what looked like little whitewashed tombs under the palm trees by the old Commissariat de Police in the grain market. Shereefa had quite a reputation even then. She swaggered around Tangier dressed half as a Moroccan woman and half as a man. She never went veiled even in those old days when all decent Moslem women still did. Shereefa could do whatever she liked because she was a hereditary saint, directly descended from the founder of a local ecstatic brotherhood. This Sufi order made him the patron saint of Tangier to whose tomb one has to take gifts in order to remain in his favour. Shereefa sold off the surplus gifts of grain, the protection money that poor country people, dirt-poor peasants, brought in. What they got back was her blessing. Like armies of ants, they came scuttling into the city with their precious wheat by the bag or the bucket or even by the handful, the spoonful to get Shereefa to give them her horny hand to kiss, her horny masculine hand. No wonder it spoiled her. By that iron hand of hers, Shereefa ruled over all the market women, the egg women and the cheese women with only one or two homemade chalk-white cottage cheeses to offer for sale on a dark green palmetto frond, the flower women and the vegetable women and the poor grubby veiled girls who hung around the bus stop to rent themselves out by the hour or the day doing housework, the maids. Not many if any of them were maidens, Shereefa saw to that. Like Cousin Antonia, she too had her Trick.

Shereefa's slick Trick was to get into the bride and take her maidenhead before the bridegroom could get to her. What with medieval Moslem Manners and Customs, this was a matter of life and death. This could be fatal. Shereefa loved that. As a practising saint, she was accustomed to play for high stakes. Besides, she was organized. To burrow right down into the red-hot heart of a wedding, a Moroccan wedding, she had built up her own all-girl music group of horrible old harridans, hags who were hired to play super-sleazy bellydance music for the sexual instruction of the bride-to-be. As a result of her slimy stratagems, a lot of these silly girls got carried away and lost their precious virginities to her and never got married at all or only much later and at a considerable discount as shopsoiled. This bellydance band of hers could grind out some hot stuff you never get to see in the movies, not even the pornos. They tell me that no Moslem man ever gets to see this kind of stuff and lives to tell of it. From the stolen glimpse I once got through a beaded curtain behind which I was hid at a friend's house, I can believe it. What I saw there was a whole lot more expert than anything Cousin Antonia's Gurls could get going in Joan of Arc's chapel.

The bride-to-be was enthroned for three days and nights, painted like a doll and wrapped up like a bundle in cloth-of-gold tissues with a gold crown on the top of it. For those three days and nights, she was supposed to just sit there soaking up this esoteric demonstration of oriental sex practices. 'Do it like this and like this and like this *to* your husband and then *with* your husband, the result is you've got him by the short hairs for life, he'll be your donkey.' The climax of this intimate instruction came when or very shortly after Shereefa whipped out her 21 centimetres and proposed to give the young virgin a demonstration on the spot. Some silly girls were taken by surprise or even by force but many another thoughtless lass became an instant lady and irreparably so, simply because she was so swept away by the delirious sway of the music that she slipped down off her throne to join in the dance. When Shereefa waltzed up to her it happened like that, zippo and rippo! Her short gasping cry was drowned out by the wild yuyuing yodels let out by the assembled ladies who carried on as if a real marriage had just been officially consummated but, well before they could think second thoughts or a traitor amongst them rush out to spread the news to the neighbours, Shereefa threw a cloak over the by now utterly unmarriageable girl and rushed her out into the street where she had a taxi throbbing, waiting for the getaway. But by the time they got out beyond the outskirts of town there would sometimes

be at least two other taxis tearing after them, one full of the baf-
fled groom and his best men, the other full of the girl's furious
father and his friends. These two cars would, ideally, crash
together and all the males would pile out to fight over the
brideprice which the groom would claim back from the father.
Shereefa just laughed.

'Hey, wake up!' Old Adam is shaking me. 'The real fun is
about to begin. For Her Holiness, this is the end of her Holy
Week on Floor Four and she is about to go into her Assumption like the BVM, the Immaculate Mary. It's a corny old trick
but a goodo one. Our Shereefa decided to do it on the stairs
out there right beneath your barred window. That's what all
the yuyuing out there is about. Well, this time she became im-
pregnated by young Yaya de la Foutaise playing the role of the
Holy Goat. Looking quite faunlike, a hairylegged young Pan
with a veil over his face, he leapt out of the duplex he inhabits
across the hall with his fat-assed terrorist dwarf. Her Holiness
was exposing herself, showing her famous 21 centimetres to
the faithful. In one single bound, Yaya was confronting her
with his equally famous 21 centimetre penis. He claims he just
wanted to see if hers really added up and that's why he slid his
along hers to see if hers really did and it didn't, not quite. Not
enough to stop him from spurting his sperm deep into her
vagina. Spitting into the palms of his hands, he cupped both
his and hers together, around both their slippery shafts. It all
happened so quick! Did he push into her or did she lean into
him, that is the question. Was his so much longer than hers
that he entered her? Nobody's talking. She slipped on something nasty on the stairs and lost her footing. She lost more
than that. His buttocks tensed and tightened. He bucked a bit
and so did she as he came in a stream that entered her sexual
sanctum sanctorum. He always claimed he liked women even
if he wasn't screwing this dwarf of his but I never thought it
would come to this when he came. At once, she became instantly pregnant.'
    'Who did? His dwarf, his tiny terrorist dwarf?'

'We'll never know about that one because she's been done in by the Thailandese transvestites. They're making chop suey out of her, can't you hear them out there? Chop chop chop! You can believe me, I'll never eat in one of those Rice Bowl restaurants again.'

'But who became pregnant, one of the transvestites or what?'

'You're still asleep. Shereefa did, Her Holiness did. It's most unusual. I've read about cases in rare medieval medical books. Violet has agreed to be the midwife when the Child comes, comes Up There on some higher floor of the Bardo we may never attain to.'

'Oh, come on now! I don't know why you say that. That's not like you in the least, Adam. With my legs, I can't count on climbing any stairs but I do intend to get the hell out of here and I will. You'll see. Don't be so damned negative.'

'Mickey Monkey is already snarling with jealousy. It's his most human characteristic. He can be dangerous. When Baby comes, someone is going to have to take care of him.'

'What makes you think it's going to be a him?'

'I meant Mickey but you're right, of course. However, no matter what sex it may be, it's going to be our Saviour, it must.'

'Now wait a minute, wait just a minute. I don't want any . . .'

'You don't want. I can't wait. Only minutes to go. Shereefa's Ultimate Assumption is about to take place. Her Holiness is going to be assumpted up on to the next floor or, who knows, even higher. I can see her out there now in that filthy stairwell, floating up up and up! It's the miracle of the Wholly Assumption all over again. Graham Greene would give his eye teeth, if he's still got them, to see this. Evelyn Wog too and all those Catholic converts. There is no precedent for this in all Moslem literature. Even the Prophet was firmly laid in his tomb in Medina beyond any possibility of another flit like the one he pulled over Jerusalem on his famous night out, bareback on his white steed winged like Pegasus. Her Holiness doesn't even have a horse. She doesn't need one.

Shereefa and Shereefa only is the Pivot of the Age. She's spinning like a top out there as she goes up up and up! This is the sacred synthesis between the sexes we've been waiting for.'

'Who's been waiting for? Not me. And I don't think the Buddhists are going to like it either.'

'Why, of course they are. At least, the Tibetans must since they're having it happen right here in their Bardo Hotel.'

'MY Hotel Bardo, please. I may be reduced to all but total impotence here in this Beckett-like burrow I've been buried in or this Burroughs-like footnote I *risk* being buried in but I insist, this is MY Beat Hotel. It cost me the earth. I had every right to have it dismantled and transported to Sunny Southern California to become one more exhibit in my Museum of Museums because it is MINE! You hear me: MINE. I'm the author and the producer and the sole director of this show and I set it right spangbang where I want it, on the San Andreas Faultline. When I go, it goes.'

'There you go again,' Adam spat at me, 'you and your almighty megalomania! You're dreaming.'

'I'm not dreaming, I'm inventing it. Writing it, if you like. Without me, the whole scheme would not exist and when I go, it goes too.'

'Well, that does sound a bit more reasonable but still recognizably schizoid. It all springs from your attitude towards women, your mother.'

'I'll thank you to leave my mother out of this. I'll take my own medicine. Women do not show up on my screen, it's that simple. Very few women have registered on my screen in my lifetime. Cousin Antonia did. She not only taught me a lot about women but about money. She sent me to her own firm of lady lawyers who got me back my money and more, lots more, an endless amount of money to spend on my dream of museums, the dream of my life. I am grateful to her, immensely. I really am. She was great.'

'That's just a mite white of you to say something nice about a woman. It may help you.'

'Help me with whom? Are you setting yourself up as my judge, doctor?'

'That's a mistake they all make. Here in the Bardo, every man is his own judge.'

'Am I supposed to feel I am lucky to be still here on trial? And you, Dr Adam, how do you stand?'

'Who, me? Me, I'm OK. Got it made and all that, wife and kids and all that, even if one of them is an ape, not an ape, some kind of monkey, I keep forgetting.'

'You seem to be losing the thread, old man.'

'I've got so much to forget, all that medical stuff and everything. Help me. Remember me something, something we've both got in common. Your choice.'

'How about remembering the first time we met, for example? I hope you're not talking about love. Love is all over the place where you'd least want to find it. Love is like the traps on a trapline strung under the snow. You don't know how it can bite until you step on to one and it springs its steel jaws and teeth on you. A friend or even an acquaintance suddenly turns on you and the last thing you expect is the reason. It's love. And it can be catching, like a virus.'

'There never was all that much love lost between us, was there? That's still another failure on your part, you know. You're supposed to be in love with your analyst. But let's not talk about that, as you say, let's not talk about that. Let's talk about your lack of love for women, the whole female sex.'

'I'm nightblind, that's all there is to it. I don't see why I should have to suffer for that. It's like astigmatism or colour blindness.'

'You're begging the question. You can't live as you have on bad terms with half of humanity and escape the heavy hand of Shereefa.'

'Humanity? Women are the Other Half of humanity, let me remind you. You can't blame me for that any more than you can blame me for my nightblindness.'

'Actually, there are more women than men. They're in the majority.'

'I know, that's what I'm afraid of.'

'And so you should be. There's worse, though. Let's look at it this way, only 10 per cent of the male population is said to be homosexual. Many of them marry. Only 1 per cent of this 10 per cent is exclusively homosexual. Think on that.'

'I do. I often do think on it with some satisfaction, don't grudge me that. But haven't we been through all this whole boring conversation before, at least a million times, over and over? You know what I think? I have come to the conclusion that, no, I am just beginning to come to the conclusion that you and I are not real people. How about that? Perhaps we are nothing more than an infinitesimally small element of a larger, much larger and all but random pattern, a very fugitive pattern like those made momentarily by schools of fish in the sea or flocks of birds in the air in which every bird and every fish plays both the follower and the leader. All those fish are one fish, one bird, one brain.'

'I get what you mean but I don't think it's an entirely novel idea, do you, hmmm? Say, by the way, do you remember what you said the other day about hearing that Mickey was writing his memoirs? Where did you hear it?'

'Hear it? Where would I hear it? Right here, right here where I am lying. Right here where I'm bound to this cot of Procrustes the Stretcher. You remember him? He stretched small people to fit his bed or he chopped off the feet of those who hung over. Out on the stairs, apparently, I heard a voice I would recognize anywhere, old Madeleine Bradley-Boyd the literary agent. She used to show up at Cousin Antonia's. A lot of those ladies wrote books. She was reading the fine print of a very long book contract to Mickey, saying things like, "My my my, young man, you certainly do know how to get what you want out of a contract, don't you?" And more of the same.'

'The sneak!'

'Who, Mickey or Madeleine? You know what it's all about?'

'It's a fake. It's a fake like Hitler's diaries, a disgusting literary fraud. Mickey can't write.'

'Who cares? You don't have to know how to write to write

books. Look at all those illiterate Moroccans who are writing books with tape-recorders. Why not our Mick? I understand he's run across, contacted and contracted an extraordinarily able ghost somewhere up there in those mysterious upper floors he frequents, an old Beatnik ghost.'

'Oh, those old Beatniks, they couldn't write themselves out of a paper bag. As Truman said: They don't write, they type. And their typing is terrible, as poor as their spelling.'

'Oh come on! How about all those books?'

'I didn't say books, I said paper bags, contracts, watertight contracts to hold all those words in and then squeeze some of the old mazoom out of them. Mickey, I must admit, knows all about that. The most useful thing we ever did for him, for him and for us, was to send him to the LSE, the London School of Economics. Not being a human, he could not be enrolled and so much the better since there's no record of it. He was allowed to sit in as an Auditor. Never missed a class. He was fascinated. Mickey took to contract law like a baboon takes to bananas, gobbled it up. No offence meant. Mickey wouldn't touch a banana, either because they are or he considers them to be too phallic to put in his mouth or for the same reason he won't touch watermelon. Racism. Reminds him of his non-human condition, something he'd sooner forget. D'ja remember anything, any details of the contract?'

'Well, enormous sums seemed about to change hands and it was all going to Mickey no matter what happened, book or no book.'

'Mark my words, there'll never be a book, never! And why should there be a book? There'll be money, lots of it but never a book. *Mickey can't write.*'

'And why should he? His life has been sufficiently glamorous, the book will write itself with a competent ghost simply hovering over a hot typewriter. I heard old Missus B-B telling him that the publisher has already sold off the foreign rights for millions and millions of dollars in fifty-five countries, including Lapland.'

'Let the Lapps lap it up, then. I'm furious. I tell you

what we'll do. When we're up there, we'll do in this ghost.'

'If you're talking in the plural and not just the imperial "we", as is your habit, you'll have to loosen my bonds here.'

'I can't do that. Only Yaya can, it's written into the plot. I mean the contract.'

'You're quite right, the ghost is written into the contract. Very clever of Mickey, old Missus B-B thought. It reads that Mick agrees to this particular ghost, named Skelton Keyes by the way, and no other. If anything happens to this particular ghost, Mick gets to keep all the money. In view of this, the publisher insists that the ghost be protected by bodyguards. Expenses for ghost to come out of royalties.'

'That must be nice work.'

'For the bodyguards?'

'No, for the ghost if he's gay. With two or more bodyguards night and day to service him, he's in clover. Well, so long now, I must be off on my mission of mercy, saving lives, ha ha ha. Toodleoo!'

I went on dreaming, of course. Sleep deserted me.

A light like a billion-watt bulb floated up through the bars on my window. The Great White Light! the Ineffable Light the Tibetans are always talking about. I was transfixed, of course. I felt I could see it, naturally, because it ran straight up my optic nerve and through the disintegrating mass of my freshly re-awakened brain right down into my hypothalamus. My narrow cell began to revolve like an old 78 rpm turntable and the bars of my window on the spiral stairs to spin past at between eight and thirteen flickers a second, the alpha rhythm of my soft old brainbox. An overwhelming flood of intensely bright abstract patterns in supernatural colours exploded somewhere behind my blind eyes where multi-dimensional kaleidoscopes whirled through endless space. Dazzling lights of unearthly brilliance and colour were developing in magnitude and complexity at great speed. Infinite acres of geometric wallpaper and rubbishy canvases by painters like Vasarely spread all around me. I was the pivot in the centre of developing worlds, giant galaxies hurtling through my own interior space at the speed of light. It all means that my EEG has not flattened out yet and the old brain is still working. I laugh uncontrollably.

Long experience of Gysin's Dreammachine in my Museum's Chapel of Extreme Experience had taught me what to expect. I had long ago learned to read these computer images to the point where they turn into dreamlike sequences like holograph movies. I knew I could expect to see the symbols of all the great world religions float free from this background noise to pass slowly and majestically across my field of vision. The Cross in all its variations flashed as brightly for me as it had for Saul on his way to Damascus racing down an avenue of trees on the buckboard of his chariot as the sun set behind the tree trunks, producing flicker at his alpha rate. So he fell off his chariot and came to as Saint Paul, more's the pity for all of us. As I said before, all these religions ought to be taxed out of existence. Then the swastikas spinning clockwise and counter were followed by a magnificently jewelled Tibetan *dorje*, raised like a club or a sceptre. The all-seeing eye of Isis floated by, eyeing me knowingly, succeeded by other eyes flashing fire. The crescent moon of Islam or the BVM and the blue hand of Fatima gave way to the symbols of forgotten religions or, who knows, those of other planets. I waited expectantly.

It was not an unmitigated delight to find Heleni Argolaki standing in front of me. She was looking good, as they say, looking like Helen of Troy or the Love Goddess or any one of those ladies. If I hadn't known the look in her eye so well, I might've thought she was glad to see me. The supreme charm of Venus was said to be her fascinating strabism. Her eyes were ever so slightly cocked so that you could never be sure exactly where she was looking. This gave her an unearthly air, an unearthly stare, so they said. Only a goddess of beauty could afford what would have been considered a fault in any ordinary girl. Helenaki achieved her effect differently. Her eyes were the colour or the colours of all the seas her ships sailed worldwide in all weathers. They could be smiling or stormy but what made them unlike all others I've ever seen was a break in the iris of her left eye which made it look, as I once told her, like a keyhole. She was furious.

Long before I could escape from Greece myself, Heleni had sailed away and gone to Lausanne to have her baby in the clinic where all good rich Greeks are born to give them Swiss nationality. If I had thought about it all, I would have suggested the States for the boy to become President like all those other bastards. I may even have said so to Cousin Antonia when I got back to Paris to tell her the whole story. She looked very grave and said, 'I suppose you *should*, but I don't think you *ought* to marry her.'

'Because of my illness, you mean?'

'No, my dear, because of your money. I'm going to send you to Washington to see my lawyers and your lawyers. Do you even know who they are? No, I thought not, nor did your mother. You have no idea of the complexity of the structures, the legal structure of my holdings and what will be yours if you handle it properly, five generations of money, big money.'

'Six, in my case. But what you say is perfectly true. All I know about it is what I read in the newspapers, what I know from my own name and number. What should I do?'

'Go see my lawyer. She'll tell you all you need to know about the dangerous network of wills and their codicils imposed upon us by our ancestors, yours and mine, and their money. One thing I can tell you is that you must not, NOT marry before you are twenty-five or you'll find yourself a pauper without a penny. All your fortune hangs on the last will and testament of a ferociously Protestant old lady you may never have heard of. Ask my lawyer, she'll tell you.'

I very nearly asked her if that went for her too. Was that why she had never married? I thought better of this and took her advice, following it almost to the letter. She advised me to go to Switzerland first to see Heleni but not to see the child unless Heleni insisted on it. When I got there she didn't. Maybe the child had already been sent to Greece, I don't really remember. Heleni was still in Switzerland because of some complications she'd had. I thought immediately of my sickness but didn't dare ask her. Antonia had advised me to offer to acknowledge the child legally, giving it dual or even triple nationality since Heleni wanted it to be Greek as well as Swiss. Since I was not Swiss, she merely thanked me gracefully. I did not offer marriage and was embarrassed to say why, over money. Like poor Mickey Monkey, I was already ashamed or at least somewhat ashamed of my money. In any case, I did not have it yet. It took all Antonia's lawyers and mine several years to fight all that through so I could start my collecting. The first thing I ever dickered for was the Acropolis and Heleni had already beaten me to it, offering her millions to have it restored under plastic or something silly. We never saw each other again from that day to this, more's the pity.

In my next analytical session with him, I told Dr Adam all about this, all. He said, 'Don't be silly. That Great White Light you saw was the fireball that followed Shereefa's aura as she was wafted upstairs, a part of her Holy Assumption. As for your syphilis, that's what got Mickey talking and singing, a syph throat.'

'Don't you mean a strep throat?'

'I mean what I say. Eva and I decided to give him clinical syphilis when we read a paper in a medical journal about the artificial induction of disease in order to produce, ah, unusual results. I may say that this was a highly underground medical journal some years old. Its publication had been suspended by the Medical Order as being quite contrary to the Hypocritic Oath and all that old-fashioned nonsense like the germ theory which Dr Burroon so rightly objects to. It was found to be financed by the Armed Citizens' Group and suspended indefinitely, if you follow me.'

'I don't want to.'

'If you don't want to follow me into space, I don't blame you. It must be beastly out there. Hope I don't have to go, ever. Anyhoo, the chancres in Mickey's larynx made it poss-

179

ible for him to talk and even to sing, made over his voice-box. I speak as a layman for your benefit. For the first time, he was able to form words, recognizable word-sounds. Until then he'd been barking like a baboon. Only Eva and I could understand him. It simply made his career, of course. You know all about that, so now for the real news. Your son is dead.'

'My son! What are you talking about?'

'Yes, your son with Helen Argolaki, he committed suicide. Went up to his mother in their villa in Kiphissia and shot himself. Put a pistol in his mouth and pulled the trigger, spattering her from head to foot with his blood and his brains.'

'When did this happen?'

'Very recently. If you hadn't been fucking about with the floors of the Bardo, he might be here by now. You'd get to know him, perhaps.'

'Oh, no!'

'Oh, yes! For all I know, he may be in California waiting for you but to meet him you'll have to be born again. If that's what you want, you'll have to leap into the next waiting womb that presents itself.'

'That's not what I want, not at all. That's got nothing to do with it. When one of those cultists asked me years ago, way back when, what I wanted, I said and I say: I want out. Out out out, understand?'

'You can't go. They've closed down the airports. Argolaki Airlines are the only ones operating.'

'You know the only thing Heleni said to me just now, back there? She said, "I've thought of you every day of my life all these years." And I said, "Why? Have you got visible scars?" I'm that awful. She'd never evacuate me, even if she could.'

'She can't. It would take another woman, entirely.'

'The very least hommage I can offer her is to say that she's the only one, the one and only, the only woman of my life. What more can she ask for?'

'She can ask for and get a whole lot more than that, the way they're settling those suits out there in California. I wish I'd

180

been a lawyer instead of a doctor, sometimes. That's what comes of Unethical Culture.'

'But what's this story about my presumptive progeny? He must have been a big boy, a man, a middle-aged man or more. Look how old I am. I feel very guilty, all of a sudden. He must have had a terrible life with her to do that at his age, don't you think. Was he normal?'

'Well, he never married, if that's what you mean.'

'I don't. I mean physically. You know what I mean. Heleni wanted him to be a mythological monster like the Minotaur.'

'That was your idea, I'm sure, knowing you as I do. People say he was a very beautiful young man, something like young Foutaise, I'm told. Spoiled rotten. Sick, you know. Maybe you missed something there.'

'Incest, you mean?'

'Well, that's highly mythological.'

'Mythology is one of the worst worn-out old tracks I know. I want to get free of that. I want to get out, as I told you. Why don't you give me a hotshot of some stuff to relieve me of myself, some carbamates for in extremis solutions. You must still have some, you're an old CIA man, aren't you?'

'I'm a medic. Not a murderer.'

'Often one and the same thing, no? But you're absolutely right, I'm not a murderee. If I had been I would have been done in long ago by some inept kidnapper, wouldn't I. How do you feel about reincarnation?'

'Yours for a better life! I'm all for it.'

'I'm not. Being born once was bad enough.'

When we are born, we start to die. The very beginning begins the end.'

'Nonsense. Who said that? First, when are we born? We begin to be born when we are conceived and when we are born nine months later we are not born all of a piece nor are we born separately, not any more than a fish in the sea in a school of fish nor a bird in the sky nor a bee in a hive. Skindiving off Algeria first brought that home to me. A school of fish is a fish. One single fish is a snack. Birds in the sky, ditto. When I was a kid on the Longfinger estate at Lost Lake in northern Montana, I saw the migrations of geese. In North Africa, I saw the arrival and departure of the storks. Follow the leader. If there is no flock, there can be no leader. One fish cannot swim alone in the sea and yet that is what I always wanted to do. To be that one fish, a loner looking for a way out through a crack in the sky, a hole in the universe through which I could get out forever. That's what attracted me so to the San Andreas Faultline when I saw a relief map of our Pacific Coast in the New York Museum of Natural History. It looked so like a sandpile on the seashore that the next wave might cause to crumble and be swept away by a storm like El Niño, the breath of a mythological manchild which wore away the shore right up to the front door of my Museum in Malibu.'

'That's too bad.'

'No, that is good. That's what I wanted. *I* called up the Tempest. I am, or I was, Duke Prospero. Like any normal child of my sort, I used to grumble that I never asked to be born. As I grew up and educated myself, I thought I might have been better born in the Italian Renaissance. I began to believe that I had been until I read what the Signore Salvati, the Chancellor of Florence, said to Ugolino Caccini in the month of May 1400 on the death of his son. He said: *Even if the soul does not die and the body is reborn, that harmonious combination that made Pietro my son has been destroyed forever.*'

'He did, did he? Intuitive ideas are difficult to modify.'

'What do you mean by that?'

'Metempsychosis is an essentially intuitive idea. There are no solid grounds on which one can base such an idea. No proofs. No nothing.'

'How about this ... all this ... our presence here? I can guess why *I'm* here. I can't imagine why *you* are or why we are seeing each other, if that's what you like to call it. We were never all that intimate. I remember the first time I ever set eyes on you without knowing who you were. Isn't that just a little bit odd that we're always meeting in hospitals?'

'No, after all I'm a doctor.'

'Yes, I remember you mumbling that when I came to and found you by my bedside in that hospital run by the Spanish nuns in Tangier. Those nuns believed pain was good for the soul, so no pain-killers. *La vida es pena*, they said to me, very Spanish. We are born to suffer. As she tore that dressing off my raw wound to which it had stuck, it was you who gave a squeak of pain, not me. I was getting used to it. You still had not given me your name when the Greek Ambassadress bustled in with her limping husband whose father had been a poet, a Nobel Prize winner. I don't know why they liked me unless because they carried on a family feud with the Argolaki clan, maybe. She brought her French chef with her to feed me up and His Excellency the Ambassador brought the Egyptian Book of the Dead, I remember. Do you think that's how I got in here?'

'I haven't the faintest idea.'

'And you?'

'Oh, one thing just led to the other. I sometimes wonder myself but I don't pore over the problem, you know. Why do you?'

'And then my Moroccan manservant came in to say that one of the more exotic ecstatic orders, the Brotherhood of the Aissaouas, was holding their week-long *moussem* up in the mountains. Every year, he and my other man Salah, the black one, used to pack up our tent and equipment to camp out up there. Besides the extremely peculiar practices of the Brothers, there was quite a licentious nightlife in the greenleaf cafés made out of branches where dancing boys shook money out of their country clients and admirers. There was no question of my going but I knew who you were by then, the notorious anti-psychiatrist, so I asked you if it would interest you to see quite a few score adepts fall into the trance dancing. You asked me how much it might cost and if they could change American Express cheques up there.'

'I deny that, categorically.'

'The title of the Egyptian Book of the Dead is: *The Book of Coming Forth by Day*, at least, that's how it is translated into

English. It really runs: RU NU PERT EM HRU. I construe that last word to be like the Arab word *Hrooj* with a soft final letter, which means coming out or going out. So the true title would be: *The Book for going out by the way of Light*, I think. I'm no scholar but I did check it with Breasted. The Clear White Light of Illumination. Don't you think that's what I saw back there?'

'If you like. Are you trying to make me suggest that you are due for a move up to Floor Five? Knowing Her Holiness only as slightly as I do, I can almost guarantee that she must have taken complete control up there. You might not like that.'

'I wouldn't. I am hoping to skip it. Besides, she wouldn't want me. I know too much. No, I was projecting a real flit, hoping to skip that stage entirely and land on Floor Six or Floor Seven or even fly right out through the roof. Surely there must be some kind of trapdoor or skylight. How about that?'

'Of course, there could be a dusty attic full of cobwebs and vampire bats, Tibetan entities, but there is said to be no roof any more, no roof at all despite the rumour that your Cousin Antonia landed on our roof by mistake when she flew back from her monastery in Japan for her very last Annual Party. Cosmic gossip maintains that when she took off in her rocket, her blast-off burned down the roof. Others claim that there never was a roof over our poor heads. The sky's the limit.'

'There is no limit. Where there is no Time, there is no limit.'

'We're still bound a bit by Time, old man. Things like that body of yours haven't gone completely to pieces, not yet. Who to believe? What is Truth? Like that poor old provincial Roman Governor, Pontius P. Pilot, wasn't it? I wash my hands of the whole matter as a sanitary precaution against idle rumour. And with that said, I must leave you, old chap, move on.'

'Cosmic gossip,' a voice whispers right into my ear, a voice with a slight foreign accent, 'cosmic gossip hath it that you are my fodder.'

For one hilarious nanosecond, I thought of snapping back, it was a male voice, that I was not his 'fodder' and he couldn't eat me. It reminded me of Cuvier, the famous French nineteenth-century naturalist whose pupils rigged themselves out in old bones one night and crept into his bedroom to scare him to death. *'Hoo hoo hoo! We're going to eat you.'* Professor Cuvier opened one eye and said sharply, 'Horns and hooves? As a graminivorous species, you can't.' On the other hand, for all I knew, this might well be one of those blood-drinking, bone-grinding Tibetan entities their holy literature is so very fond of: *'licking human brains, drinking blood, wrenching heads from corpses, tearing out hearts: thus will they come, filling the worlds.'* Just in time, I did remember that these were mainly goddesses holding blood-filled skull-bowls: *'Dark-Green Ghasmari drinking blood with majestic relish, the Yellow-White Chandali wrenching a head from a corpse, her right hand holding a heart, her left putting the corpse in her mouth and eating it, Dark-Blue Smasha tearing asunder a head from a corpse and eating it.'* This was far from the fibrefree diet the good Dr Adam had promised me and besides, it sounds very anti-feminist. *'The Yellow Bat-Headed Delight-Goddess holding a shaving knife in her hand.'* We all know what she holds that in her hand for, castration, making men into eunuchs. Delight-Goddess, indeed! I could feel my tired old balls retract up into my abdomen in a helluva hurry. How could they ever have made a son for me?

My good judgement advises me: Say nothing. Do nothing. Hold nothing. Just lie there, lie doggo. *'Thy goal is the Unbecome, the Unborn, the Unmade, the Unformed.'* In my circumstances and in my condition, I have found this impossibly difficult.

'I have come to help you.' What worrisome words! His sibilant whisper tickles the hairs of my ear unbearably, like a gnat caught in the trap of my ear. I'd give anything to work my little finger in there.

'Help?' I murmur miserably. I mean to say, I don't want any of your fucking help, thank you very much. Go away. Mind your own business. Just leave me alone, willya!

'Yes, yes,' he hisses, 'you have only to do what I tell you.'

I groan. The young are like that, they always seem to think they know better than you do what you want, you old fogey. The young are insufferably bossy.

'I've come to release you from your restraint. Please excuse these cold metal hands. I lost my own playing with firecrackers. These are my stainless steel prostheses. I can handle them pretty well for this kind of work but some things I could do before my accident I can't do any more, like roll a good joint, for instance. You don't happen to have a stash of hash on you, do you?'

I roll my head around as indignantly as I can in negation. Anyone attending my deathbed or worse should bring his own stuff, his own shit, I am very tempted to tell him. Can't he see what a state I'm in after twenty, twenty-five days dead. Twenty-eight? I am furious.

Can't this apparently well-intentioned young man with stainless steel hands just have pity! I really don't want him to revive me. I am too far gone. Doesn't he realize what happens to an old body? A rotten old body that's falling apart isn't worth saving. All the protein that glued me together has fled. My skin is flaking and peeling off me like parchment. Nothing is left of my muscle but dried sinew, cordage. I've been here too long. My name isn't Lazarus and even he ... migawd! Just think what poor old Laz' must have looked and smelled like at that fancy funeral party when they pulled him out of his coffin. Muttering burlap, mumbling, 'Thank you, Master, thank you.' Not me. I don't intend to go to one single more party, ever. I don't want to go back to Capri or Positano or even Capistrano as a swallow. I mean to get out of here and come back again never! Heavenly reunions with one's Loved One? Ugh! There is no one I ever knew in this world I want to see again.

A story like this can have no happy ending.

Or can it?